KING OF RASCALS

ROB LINK

2011 Reformed Church Press

Copyright © 2011 by Reformed Church Press

All rights reserved. No portion of this book may be reproduced, stored in a retrieval system, or transmitted in any form or by any means—electronic, mechanical, photocopy, recording, scanning, or other—except for brief quotations in critical reviews or articles, without the written permission of the publisher.

Unless otherwise noted, Scripture quotations are from the HOLY BIBLE NEW INTERNATIONAL VERSION. Copyright © 1973, 1978, 1984 by International Bible Society. Used by permission of Zondervan Publishing House. All rights reserved.

Scripture quotations marked NLT are taken from the Holy Bible, New Living Translation, copyright © 1996, 2004, 2007. Used by permission of Tyndale House Publishers, Inc., Carol Stream, Illinois 60188. All rights reserved.

Dedication

To my five wonderful children: Jake, Max, Zeke, Reese, and Eesie. I love you guys more than you'll ever know. My prayer is that you know the King of Rascals and know that you are royalty.

King of Rascals

Introduction 7

Part 1

Chapter 1   The King of Rascals..9
Chapter 2   Rascal Healer...19
Chapter 3   Ultimate Rascal 27
Chapter 4   Fig Tree Religion 37
Chapter 5   Geckos and Grace..45
Chapter 6   The Stinky Gate and the Pool of Slim Chance...............53
Chapter 7   Canaanites and Aristotle................................67
Chapter 8   Lewis's Logic..75

Part 2

Chapter 1   No More Kate the Commoner 83
Chapter 2   This Is Jericho 91
Chapter 3   Her Royal Highness.....................................101
Chapter 4   Be That Priest..113

King of Rascals

Introduction

If you don't know much about Jesus this book is for you.

If you've known Jesus for decades and are still trying to figure out who he is, this book is for you.

If you've never been to church before and wouldn't know when to stand or when to sit, this book is for you.

If you've spent your entire life in the church and know the routine like the back of your hand, this book is for you.

If you want to know Jesus, I've written this book just for you.

I want people to know Jesus.

Not Jesus the way many misguided Christians portrayed him: angry, grumpy, ready to singe sinners with a bolt of lightning.

Not the cartoonish Jesus: a white guy with vague, mystical eyes who wears a flowing, pure white gown and sandals and sits on a cloud all day with perfectly coiffed hair.

I want people to know the real Jesus.

The Jesus found in the Bible.

Jesus is so often mis-portrayed that it's no wonder so many people turn away from him.

We live in a free country—thank God. We do not live in a theocracy. Everyone has a choice whether they embrace or reject Jesus. Unfortunately it's become easy to reject Jesus as he's portrayed in popular culture (angry or begowned).

I want people to know the Jesus revealed in the Scriptures.

The Jesus found there is attractive and appealing.

I want to tell you about the real Jesus, not some unintentionally or intentionally misrepresented Jesus.

Arguably, the number one reason that churches—communities of believers—exist is to show people who Jesus is.

A believer's job is to tell people about the God of the scriptures so that they can either reject him or embrace him.

This book is my offering to that end. I hope it helps you see him and maybe show him to others.

King of Rascals Part 1

Chapter 1

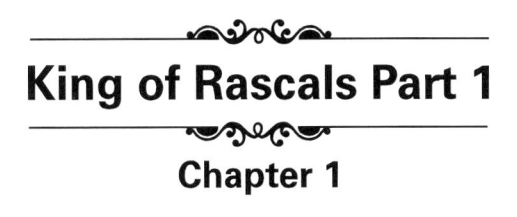

The King of Rascals

By definition a rascal is a rogue, a scoundrel.

One dictionary defines "rascal" this way: a scalawag; prone to mischief, to disobedience.

Rascal.

The apostle Paul says in the third chapter of the book of Romans: "All have sinned and fallen short of God's standard." Rascals.

Isaiah in the Old Testament, chapter 53, says that all of us like sheep have gone astray. Each of us has turned to our own way. Rascals.

Here's the fact of the matter. We are all a bunch of rascals. You're a rascal. I'm a rascal. The Bible teaches that we are all rogues, scoundrels, and scalawags. We are all rascals.

We need to get this through our thick skulls. We are rascals. We have sinned and fallen short. All of us have gone astray. Rascals.

You.

And me.

Rascals.

However, this book isn't about us. It isn't about our rascal status.

It's about Jesus.

The King of Rascals.

Jesus? The King of Rascals? Let me explain.

In the New Testament books of First Timothy and Revelation, Jesus is called King of kings and Lord of lords. He is king of everything. And if he is the king of everything, he is the King of Rascals.

Who is the king of glory, the Lord, strong and mighty? Who is this King of Rascals? Jesus. That's who.

Your King.

And mine.

In this book we're going to learn about or be reminded about the King of kings and Lord of lords. Jesus. The King of Rascals.

Here's something that might be shocking: Jesus really likes rascals.

A whole lot!

And since we're all rascals, that's great news.

Look in the scriptures and you'll learn about the knuckleheads that Jesus chose to partner with to advance his kingdom. He chose a bunch of illiterate, smelly, stinky, backwoods, uneducated, religiously uncouth fishermen.

Rascals.

The King of Rascals has a warm spot in his heart for all rascals.

Including you.

And me.

(Feel free to smile at this good news.)

I invite you to learn or relearn who Jesus is by learning about what he said and did. You may choose to reject Jesus, but at least you'll be making an informed decision. Too many people have rejected a misrepresented Jesus. Or maybe even worse, many others have been following the wrong Jesus—the angry Jesus, or the sitting-on-a-cloud Jesus.

Let's look a bit closer at the Jesus often portrayed in our churches today.

Jesus is often presented as one of two extremes. One Jesus is boring and predictable; he's pale and fragile looking, always perfectly groomed, and walks around surrounded by a few tame sheep and looking up toward heaven...*yawn*. As author Dorothy Sayers puts it, "We have declawed the lion of Judah [a name for Jesus] and made him a housecat for pale priests and pious old ladies." Yuck.

At the other extreme, Jesus is portrayed as "angry man." Have you seen the movie *Elf*? Remember the angry elf, Miles Finch? (If you've not yet seen *Elf*, for the betterment of your life, you probably ought to.) Jesus is often seen as Miles Finch's double. He's angry Jesus. Ready to smite somebody. He's got that lightning bolt and is ready to strike you down at a drop of a moral. Yikes.

Maybe you've had a hard time accepting Jesus or telling others about him because he's been presented as either of these extremes. But I promise you, these caricatures have little to do with the Jesus of scripture. The King of Rascals is so much more.

So let's get a clear understanding of who it is we are worshiping or who we're rejecting.

Who is this King of Rascals?

We'll start with the first time Jesus walks in. It's recorded in the book of John, chapter 2, the first 11 verses: "...a wedding took place in Cana in Galilee. Jesus' mother was there, and Jesus and his disciples also had been invited to the wedding."

Jesus and his disciples had been invited to a wedding.

Hang on right there.

Really? Come on! I mean, based on much of my childhood imagery of Jesus, this mystical guy surrounded by sheep, I wouldn't have invited him to a party. He would bore everyone to death. I wouldn't have invited angry Jesus either—he'd be sure to kill the party's mojo!

But in the book of John we learn that the King of Rascals was quick to get his party on. Or let me say it this way: Jesus was a center of joy that spilled over to other people.

In a book I read recently, the author talks about the story of Lazarus. You know, he was dead for three days, Jesus came, called him out of the tomb, and he came running out. The author said Jesus didn't call Lazarus out of the tomb to live a melancholy, stoic life. He called him to life! He called him to joy.

The fact that Jesus was someone people invited to the party shows us that Jesus was a man who shared their joy. Maybe uptight followers of Jesus need to just relax a bit. Or even better, maybe we should just party.

The Old Testament tells us that a cheerful heart is good medicine (Proverbs 17:22). Clearly this King of Rascals was good medicine.

A while back Kristy, my wife, and I were on a plane traveling to our vacation destination. On the airplane we met the woman who was seated next to Kristy. It was instantly clear that she loved Jesus and was passionate for the Word of God. She was a sister in the Lord. But as we talked it became clear that she knew very little about joy. When she found out I was a pastor and Kristy was a solid believer in Jesus, she began drilling Kristy. "Well, do you know what your purpose in life is right now?" "Well, what version of the Bible do you use?" "The NIV? That is the devil's tool."

This poor woman did not know the joy of the Lord. She kept peppering Kristy with questions. "Do you have the Holy Spirit in your life?" Yeah, I do. "Do you speak in tongues?" No. "Then you don't have the Spirit." She was just so uptight about believing her perfect little doctrine on some disputable biblical matters—"NIV or King James?"—that she forgot the King of Rascals is about joy.

I guess I wasn't feeling the joy either, because my prayer was that I wouldn't smack her. I was hoping that the people around us would not hear her, because she was just so angry and uptight. She looked like angry Jesus. And who needs more of that! There was something missing in the Jesus she knew. Her Jesus would not have been invited to the party.

So here is a question for all you Christians out there: do people ever ask, "Why are you so happy?" Have you ever responded, "Man, I was in the presence of God today" or "I was at church this morning"?

I'd imagine for many of us this rarely happens. Yet there is something about the joy of being with Jesus that is contagious. If the point of it all is to help people know the King of Rascals, we need to grow deep-rooted joy in our hearts. Jesus went to the party. And he calls us to be party people.

Joy! Maybe we need to rediscover our joy in Christ. Maybe we need a reintroduction to this King of Joy.

Here's another question: how many of us experience Sunday morning church more like a trip to the proctologist than to a party?

Right off the bat in our wedding story, in the gospel of John, we learn that this King of Rascals is about joy. So maybe if we don't laugh out loud when we're at church we have missed something.

Joy.

Back to the wedding in Cana. Jesus' mother was there. The wine ran out, and Jesus' mother said to him, "They have no more wine." "Dear woman," he responds. "Why do you involve me? My time has not yet come."

(Now we need to be careful here. Jesus is not saying, "Woman, leave me alone." "Dear woman," in the Hebrew culture that Jesus was a part of, is a phrase that is respectful and kind. I don't want anyone to start calling their mother "woman.")

So when the wine was gone, Jesus' mother said to him, "They have no more wine."

Stop right there.

How many of you married folks had an open bar or wine at your wedding? Many weddings today, especially Christian weddings, do not include alcoholic beverages. So we might read this and think, so what if the wine ran out? But the original hearers of the story were Hebrews; the context is Jewish. Hebrew people's culture was quite different from ours.

One ancient rabbi said, "There is no joy without wine."

We need to understand the cultural context of this story. According to ancient records, the wine offered at a wedding in Jesus' time on earth was two parts wine to three parts water. So it wasn't a strong drink. And it wasn't just the drink that brought the joy. In Hebrew culture wine was a symbol of life because it was made from the fruit of the living vine that God created.

Throughout Hebrew scripture and culture wine was an important symbol of life. And without life there is no joy. For a groom at his wedding, which usually lasted seven days, it would be very humiliating to run out of wine. The symbol of life would be gone. People would begin to say, "Uh oh, this marriage is hosed."

This was no small matter for Jesus' mother to say, "Hey, we are out of wine." This was a big deal, which is why she says to the servants, "Do whatever Jesus tells you to do."

And what does Jesus tell them to do?

Nearby stood six water jugs, the kind used for ceremonial washing, each holding twenty to thirty gallons. Jesus told the servants, "Fill the jars with water…draw some out and take it to the master of the banquet."

The master of the banquet tasted the water that Jesus had changed into wine. The banquet master called the groom over and said, "You saved the best wine for last."

Stop right there!

We learn something about the King of Rascals when we see him tackle this wedding conundrum: your problems, whether deep and heavy or light and superficial, matter to him.

Your problems.

They matter to him.

This is good news, my friends. Let me help you grasp the goodness by asking you a question.

Do you have a pulse? Then you've got issues. You're a rascal. No matter what problem you happen to be in—whether it's a humiliating experience, a wayward son or daughter, a marriage on the rocks, financial ruin, unemployment, addictions haunting you, a sick parent, whatever it is—your problem happens to be something the King of Rascals cares about.

This is good news.

The apostle Peter says, "Cast your cares on him [Jesus]." Why? "Because he cares for you." We learn in this wedding miracle of Jesus that no problem is too small or too big. He will notice. And he will care. After all, he has a soft spot in his heart for rascals.

Back to the story.

Here's something else we learn about the King of Rascals. The six stone water jars that had held water and now held wine were the kind that Jewish people used for ceremonial washing.

How many jars were there? Six. For us, numbers are all about quantity: six means six. But for Hebrew people, the number six also had a deeper level of meaning. In Hebrew culture the number that expressed perfection was the number seven.

But if something was not perfect, they would assign it a number close to the perfect number. This was a way of stating that something was imperfect, a shallow imitation, seeming to be close to perfect but in reality far from it. The Hebrew people had a number that perfectly represented the imperfect, the tarnished, the not-quite-there, the not good enough. Any guess what that number was? That's right, six.

So when a Hebrew person hears that Jesus used six jars when he turns water into wine, it tells them that the King of Rascals chose to use something imperfect to bring about his miracle.

Did you catch that? The King of Rascals uses that which is imperfect to bring about a miracle.

And if you're a rascal, someone who is far from perfect, this is good news. Because in choosing six jars Jesus says, I am going to use imperfect rascals like you to do my work, just like I did back then.

Warm up to that a little bit! This is great news.

Do you remember what those jars were used for? Ceremonial washing.

The Hebrew people were very tidy; they had lots of rules about cleanliness. Things that were "unclean" would never be used for "clean" activities. Jars used for ceremonial washing were certainly not appropriate to drink from. If the master of the banquet had known that the really good wine he had just been sipping came out of washing jars he would have been mortified. He probably would have fired the servants after flogging them. Because you don't mix the clean with the unclean.

So we learn something else about the King of Rascals. He uses unclean vessels to accomplish great things.

Let me make it plain. Jesus uses unclean, set aside, less than good, not very special items to do remarkable things.

Listen here, you rascal. Jesus wants to use you. The King of Rascals wants to use you to change your family, your neighborhood, and maybe your whole town or city.

Let's review: The King of Rascals is about joy. The King of Rascals is concerned about all of your problems. And the King of Rascals uses ordinary, imperfect people to do great things.

Here's another observation about the wedding story. Jesus' instructions to the servants—to fill up the jars, draw out some wine, and take it to the master of the banquet—his instructions are followed by three wonderful words: They did so.

Without these three words, without the servants' "doing," there would have been no miracle. A wedding party would not have been blessed. The groom would have been humiliated. A marriage would have gotten off on the wrong foot.

Without "They did so," the glory of the Lord, as it is says in verse eleven, would not have been revealed. We would not have been talking about this wedding at all. "They did so."

When the servants of the King of Rascals do what he tells them to do, his glory is revealed. Miracles happen. People are blessed. When the servants of the King of Rascals do what the King of Rascals says to do, the glory of the Lord is revealed.

Let's do what he tells us to do, and see what he does! Through our imperfect selves, when we obey the King of kings and Lord of lords, amazing things will happen. You might feel like a rascal, but the reality is that you're a miraculous vessel when you partner with this king of rascals.

When the master of the banquet tasted the miracle wine, he did not realize where it had come from (lucky for the servants!), but the servants who brought him the wine knew. The emcee calls the bridegroom aside and says, "Everyone brings out the choice wine first and then the cheaper wine after the guests have had too much to drink; but you have saved the best till now." You have saved the what? The best. This reveals one more thing about the King of Rascals that is pretty beautiful.

The parents of a close friend of mine were telling me about a gift they had given to their grandson on his birthday. Legos. Their facial expressions showed how excited they had been to give him the Lego set. Not just any Lego set. It was one of those big ones that probably cost too much. But they said the cost didn't mean anything to them—it was their grandson's birthday and they wanted to give him this pretty sweet gift. Because he got this lavish, unbelievably unexpected gift, when their grandson opened up this massive Lego set he just fell over and started beating his hands and feet on the ground in happiness. He was overwhelmed by the generosity and goodness of grandma and grandpa.

It's a great illustration of the heart of the King of Rascals. In one of his teachings, to a crowd that gathered to hear him speak (John, chapter 2), Jesus asked, "If your son asked for a fish would you give him a snake? Or if your child asked for a piece of bread, would you give him a stone?" He knew the answer was, Of course not! And he went on to say, "If you're a rascal, and yet you know how to give good gifts to your children, how much more does your heavenly Father love to give you good gifts?"

Jesus didn't just turn water into wine, he turned water into great wine. The King of Rascals loves to give generously, ungrudgingly, and lavishly to his children. Now let me connect the dots for you. So you can be happy about this news.

The apostle Paul said that God destined us to be adopted as his children. John says (1 John, chapter 3): "See what great love the Father has lavished on us, that we should be called children of God! And that is what we are!"

The point I am making is really good news! The King of Rascals loves to lavish great, wonderful, and glorious gifts on his kids!

On you!

There is good stuff for you because the King of Rascals loves to give to you. The King of Rascals could have given okay wine. But that wasn't good enough. Because the King of Rascals loves to bless us beyond our expectations.

This King of Rascals seems pretty cool to me. Yet this is just the beginning. We have much to learn about who Jesus really is.

Chapter 2

Rascal Healer

Jesus is the King of Rascals. Thank God Almighty for that.

Let's look at the King's interaction with a rascal whose story we find in Mark,` chapter 1, verses 40 to 45. It's a story about Jesus' encounter with a leper.

Before we get to the story a fact or two about leprosy might be helpful.

Leprosy in ancient days was considered a death sentence. It was a death sentence both physically and socially. If you had leprosy, your life was as good as over. People with leprosy experienced disfigurement of their skin and bones. Arms and legs twisted, fingers curled into claws, and noses collapsed.

In advanced leprosy the nervous system is affected. All pain receptors that go to the brain are shut off. You feel no pain, nothing at all, even when you're walking around and step on something sharp. You cut your foot and you never even know you've done it. If you pick up something that's extremely hot you can't feel a thing. You don't know that you're injured and your injuries become infected. The infections get so bad you lose parts of your body.

People can't stand to look at you, and they're afraid they will catch what you have. Even though you can't feel physical pain, you still feel the deep emotional pain of being alone and unwanted. (I recommend Philip Yancey and Paul Brand's *Pain: The Gift Nobody Wants* for more on the topic of leprosy.)

People with leprosy in ancient days were banished from the community. They were on the outside of public life. If they were ever to walk in public they would have to holler out, "Unclean! Unclean!" so everyone around them would know to stay away.

Can you imagine living life that way? When people see you coming, they scatter. That's intense isolation. You have a contagious disease. So touching you makes others unclean as well. Even in our culture today, what are we taught in first aid? If we see any injury, what's the first thing we are supposed to do? Put on latex gloves. We don't want our skin touching their skin, touching their blood. So magnify that times a hundred with a leper.

You just do not touch a leper.

We have a parallel in our culture.

It's called shame.

And it's equally as deadly. If not more so.

Shame is a multifaceted beast. It can come from others. It can come from ourselves. Which is to say, it can come from the outside or the inside. Either way it is a killer of souls.

Just ask the poor kid at school whose single mom can't afford the latest styles.

Just ask the divorced man or woman in many a church.

Just ask the overweight person—man or woman.

Just ask the guy who keeps visiting porn sites even though deep down he doesn't want to.

Just ask the woman whose husband keeps visiting porn sites.

Just ask the alcoholic.

The homeless.

The unemployed.

Just ask the lady riddled with depression.

The kid who isn't athletic enough, you know, the last one chosen.

Just ask the one who's been sexually abused.

The wife who has been beaten.

The husband who has been browbeaten.

I could go on. Shame is deadly. Worse than leprosy.

Just ask…yourself. You know, don't you? If you're honest with yourself, you know. Deep down there is that thing that you hope no one finds out. That thing you keep buried deep in your closet—so deep, in fact, you may not have any conscious awareness of it. But the shame is there.

Worse than leprosy.

Mark, chapter 1, verse 40, tells us that a man with leprosy came to Jesus and begged him on his knees to heal him: "If you are willing, you can make me clean."

This guy was far gone with leprosy. He probably had a sunken-in nose, hands like claws. He was probably missing toes and fingers, maybe even whole limbs…not a pretty sight.

He was a rascal. An untouchable rascal.

He was a total outcast, isolated and alone.

The social rules of the day said he needed to stay away from others.

But when he saw Jesus, he thought to himself, *Forget the rules! I'm going to go to Jesus. I'm going to plead my case on my knees.*

This man with leprosy, this outcast, this rascal, runs to Jesus.

He goes to Jesus in complete humility, begging on his knees.

Little did he know this was the best place for a rascal to be.

The guy knew his condition. Everyone around him knew his condition. Jesus knew his condition. There was no way to hide his condition.

The way the leper came to Jesus shows us something about our approach to Jesus.

There is no need to approach the King of Rascals pretending we have our act together.

The King knows otherwise.

And loves us anyway.

He loves rascals.

Too often in our culture, we try to hide our filth.

A leper couldn't hide it.

But we do. Or at least we try.

In my book *Pulse*, I speak strongly of the need for us to live authentically—both with ourselves and with others. The constant hiding of our sin and filling our closet with secrets and shame is literally killing us. There is something life giving, something freeing about coming to Jesus like this leper.

When we approach Jesus we need to remember that he knows us better than we know ourselves. There is no need to hide. Let's approach him like the leper. Honest, raw, and real.

This might seem contradictory to the way we've been trained to go through life. After all, we learn at a young age that when people ask us how we are doing, the right answer is "Fine." Most people don't really want to know how we are, so we better just pretend all is well even if it isn't.

Yet as counterintuitive as it may seem, the leper's approach is the right one. It's the first step toward healing and freedom.

Back to the story.

Here's another thing about this guy.

The leper knew Jesus.

But not really.

We know this because he says to Jesus, *If you're willing*, you can make me clean. He realizes Jesus *can* make him clean. He knows the power of Jesus. When he heard about Jesus he broke all the rules and said, "This King of Rascals, this guy can heal me." So he knew that about Jesus.

But he says, "If you're willing," which tells us that he didn't really know Jesus.

Listen. Jesus is not only able but *willing* to make every rascal clean.

Jesus is willing to make every rascal clean.

Everyone.

That is the power of his death and his coming back to life. Before he died on the cross, taking on himself all of our leprosy, our sin, and our shame, Jesus said, "It is finished." It's finished! He's taken it all. If we, like the leper, approach him with our junk, he'll take it and call it done.

He says, "Come to me and I *will* make you clean! Because it's finished. I've done it. I've taken away your sin. Come to me and be free."

In Luke, chapter 4, when Jesus said he has come to heal the brokenhearted (NKJV)—he meant it!

When the prophet Joel promised that the Lord would restore the years the locust had eaten—he meant it!

When Jesus said "I am with you always"—even in the middle of your shame—he meant it!

Many translations of verses 41 and 42 of Mark, chapter 1, say Jesus was filled with compassion for the man with leprosy. Filled with compassion, Jesus reached out his hand and touched the man. He said, "I'm willing. Be clean." And immediately the leprosy left the man. And he was cured.

Now wait a minute. Did you notice that? Before the man was healed, Jesus touched him.

I imagine that Jesus could have just spoken a word and the dude would've been healed.

There are other stories of Jesus healing people without a touch.

But not in this story.

In large part, the touch was part of the healing.

Remember in Jesus' culture lepers were untouchable. They had to avoid contaminating others by never touching them. There were strict rules that kept this man away from physical contact with others. Most likely it had been years since he had been touched.

Jesus touched him.

When no one else would.

Wow. Almost makes me want to weep when I think of how icky I've felt at times, or when I see folks the world spurns.

Jesus touched him.

When no one else would.

A first-century leper is not beyond the touch of the King of Rascals.

Neither is a twenty-first-century rascal like me or you.

Wow.

No matter what you have heard, you are the one the Lord wants to touch with his healing, kind, affectionate hand.

Those voices inside your head are wrong.

Those hateful voices from others are wrong.

You are the one the King of Rascals came to heal.

With a touch.

That's pretty cool. Think about it. The world we live in likes to define who's in and who's out, who's cool and who's not, who's hip and who's not. This is deadly and the cause of much shame.

In addition to that we like to define people by their past and dole out status or a lack of it because of the deeds of yesterday. Yuck.

In the face of this prevalent nonsense the King of Rascals reaches out his hand to touch and to heal.

This is good news for you. In the presence of the King of Rascals there is freedom for you.

This is good news for others. If more people knew of this reality, more people would walk into freedom.

So here is what I recommend.

Pretend you are a leper living in a land of lepers and approach Jesus asking for his healing touch.

Chapter 3

Ultimate Rascal

John, chapter 4, says, "Now [Jesus] had to go through Samaria. So he came to a town in Samaria called Sychar, near the plot of ground Jacob had given to his son Joseph. Jacob's well was there, and Jesus, tired as he was by his journey, sat down by the well. It was about noon."

When a Samaritan woman came to the well to get water, Jesus said to her, "Will you give me a drink?" The woman said, "You are a Jew and I am a Samaritan woman. How can you ask me for a drink?"

It was a good question.

Jews did not associate with Samaritans.

A first-century Jewish person would have understood some things about this encounter that you and I miss today. The first thing we miss is the significance of the place where the encounter takes place—Samaria.

The original hearers—the Jewish folks way back then, and the Gentile people, the non-Jews—would read this text and say to themselves, "Hold on—Jesus had to go through *Samaria*?"

The text says that Jesus "*had to* go through Samaria" (italics added). Someone living in Judea in the first century would hear this and say, "Oh my goodness. This is scandalous!" And it was. Because of something that had happened way back in roughly 720 B.C.

That's when the army of the Assyrian nation swept down into Jerusalem and conquered the nation of Israel. The Assyrians took many if not most of the Israelites back to Assyria, leaving only a small number of Jews behind. The Assyrians made the Jews their slaves and treated them brutally.

The Assyrians worshiped idols. Yet the captive Jews hung on to their belief in the one true God. They followed the teachings found in what we now call the Old Testament, and they refused to be swept into the culture of the Assyrian idol worshipers. And it cost them dearly.

Meanwhile, while this was going on with the bulk of Jews, a group of Jews who had not been taken into captivity and who were living in a region called Samaria said, "Forget the teachings of our fathers to stay separate from other peoples. It's too hard."

The Jews in Samaria intermarried with the people around them. They said, "We are going to take the things of Judaism that we like, but we'll also take religious stuff from these other people who worship idols. We're going to make our own hybrid religion; we're going to do our own thing."

When the enslaved Jews were released after hundreds of years in captivity, they were repulsed by the Jews in Samaria—people who had married people who were not Jewish and who mixed the Jewish religion with idol worship. The Jews who had stayed faithful for centuries to the one true God in spite of captivity and slavery regarded the descendents of the Jews who had remained in Samaria as religiously impure and racially unclean.

The racial tension between the Jews and Samaritans of Jesus' day was every bit as bad as the tension between whites and blacks in the 1950s in America. One rabbi of Jesus' time calls the Samaritans half-bloods because their Jewish blood was mixed with Assyrian blood.

You may have heard another story about a Samaritan that's in the Bible. It's in Luke, chapter 10. One day Jesus told his followers that the greatest commandment of all is to love God and your neighbor. Someone in the crowd of followers asked Jesus, "Who do you mean when you say 'your neighbor'"? Jesus answered the question by telling a story, and a Samaritan man is the hero of the story.

Jesus said, "Suppose a dude is walking down a deserted stretch of road, gets assaulted and beat up, and is left in the ditch to die. A priest walks by, sees the man, and goes right on by. A teacher comes by and sees the man, and he too goes on his way. Then a Samaritan man comes along, and he stops and helps the guy. The Samaritan picks the guy up, puts him on his donkey, and takes him to an inn. He pays the innkeeper to take care of this dude and gives extra money for a room and any additional costs that may come up. So who is the good neighbor?"

The Jews answered, "The one who took care of him."

They couldn't even bear to say "the Samaritan." They were in shock that Jesus had used a Samaritan as the hero of the story, since the Jews and the Samaritans were at odds, racially and religiously.

The Jews so hated the Samaritans that if a Jewish boy married a Samaritan girl, the family of the boy would hold his funeral and treat the son as dead from then on.

Going back to the story of the Samaritan woman at the well, we can see why Jewish people would read this text, and say, "He *had to* go through Samaria?" They would say, "Oh, no, he didn't." In fact, every Jew in that time would have taken a six-day trip around Samaria because they wouldn't even set foot in the region.

So Jewish people in Jesus' time would be saying, "No, Jesus didn't have to go through Samaria. He could have walked around it like everyone else does."

Jewish people would also have been offended to hear that Jesus struck up a conversation with a woman. We read this today and it's no big deal that Jesus talks to a woman. As a man, I talk to women all the time. It's common practice in our day and age. No big deal. Jesus is talking to a woman. Who cares?

We miss how radical it was for Jesus to talk with a woman. Women in Jesus' day were treated like possessions. A woman could not vote and had no say in public life. A woman literally was to be seen and not heard. Women were way down on the social totem pole. In that culture an eight-day-old baby boy was more worthy of respect than an adult woman.

If you read the books of Leviticus and Exodus (and if you can do it without falling asleep), you will find passages that say that if someone accidently kills a man, the one who did the accidental killing will have to pay the man's family about eight thousand dollars. But if someone accidentally kills a woman, her family only needs to be paid about half that amount. In every way, a woman was worth much less than a man. How do you like that? Kinda stinks, right?

The point is, no Jewish male, and especially a rabbi, a teacher, like Jesus, would ever begin a conversation with a woman. It would be way beneath his dignity.

But Jesus asked the woman for a drink from the well. Shocking.

He went on to tell her he could give her living water, and if she drank it she would never be thirsty again.

"Sir, give me this water so that I won't get thirsty and have to keep coming here to draw water," she says.

Jesus continues the conversation. He says, "Go and get your husband and come back."

She says, "I have no husband."

Jesus says, "That's right. The fact is you have had five husbands. And the man you are with now is not your husband."

Of course the woman was blown away that he knew all this about her.

The woman had been married five times, and now she was living with a sixth guy. You might be thinking, well that's a lot of relationships, but it happens. Today more than half of marriages end in divorce, and it's common for children in a family to have different fathers or mothers. In this culture divorces are a dime a dozen, they happen all the time. Although even today five divorces would be a lot.

In the time of Jesus a woman who was divorced was considered used goods, worthless, to be discarded. Back then a woman found her worth in two ways: having a husband and bearing male children. A woman who was divorced was absolutely worthless in that culture, rejected by society, an outcast, spurned relationally. The type of man who would marry such a woman would not have been a man of high character. He would likely be an abusive man, a man who treated her poorly. And this had happened five times. She was a lonely, hurting person who was probably living with someone just to be with a warm body, just to find someplace to connect with another human being.

She was a rascal to be sure. A very lonely rascal.

Do you remember what time of day was it when Jesus met the Samaritan woman at the well? It was noon. That's something else about the story that is out of step with life back then. Women didn't gather water at noon, at the hottest time of day. The times for gathering water were early in the morning or late in the evening when it was nice and cool. This woman went at noon because no one else would be there. She was someone the other women despised because she was divorced many times, and now she was living with someone she wasn't married to. She went at noon to avoid the icy stares of the other women. She couldn't handle that rejection. Although she would have been in the company of others in the morning or evening, she still would have been utterly alone in a way that would burn and hurt deeply. At least at noon it would be hot on the outside, but a little cooler on the inside.

Understanding the background and knowing a little about the King of Rascals, we begin to see why Jesus *had to* go through Samaria.

He had to go through Samaria because when the King of Rascals sees a place of racism, sexism, and religious persecution, he walks straight into it, not around it.

He confronts it head on and says, "This is wrong!"

Throughout history, Jesus' teachings have inspired people to take a stand against racial and social injustice.

For example, the slave trade was ended by Christ followers, beginning with William Wilberforce in England. Wilberforce wanted to be a missionary; he loved Jesus deeply. But the Lord said, "You are not to leave your place in Parliament. You are not becoming a missionary; you are going to bring the voice of Jesus in this culture, in Parliament, and convince people that slavery is wrong, racism is wrong, oppressing people because they're of a certain ethnicity is wrong." (Watch the 2006 movie *Amazing Grace* to learn more.)

Jesus' going straight through Samaria is his way to say racism and oppression are just wrong. He was taking a stand against it. When the King of Rascals saw ethnic tension, he said, "No, the kingdom of God is not about this." Jesus did not say in Matthew 28, "Go and make disciples of people who look just like you." It does not say in the book of Revelation, "In eternity, you'll be worshiping with just one nation and one tribe." Jesus said, "Go and make disciples of all nations," and Revelation shows us that people from every nation, tongue, and tribe will worship God together.

Jesus sees ethnic division and says, "No, it's gotta stop!"

The King of Rascals. Are you his follower? Followers do what the one they are following does. Have you taken a stand against ethnic and racial tension? Have you said racism is wrong? How about sexism? Stand for what he stood for and against what he stood against. The King had to go through Samaria because he had to make a stand.

Here's a fact: white people, simply because they are white, have privileges that people of color do not have.

Because I am a white man, I am much more likely to get a home loan than someone with my education who is an African American. This is not right.

My friend Tim, who is white, can go shopping in any store and be left alone. But when my friend Julio, a Hispanic guy with the same education, same kind of job, walks through a store, he is much more likely to be followed by employees simply because of the color of his skin. Tim's wife, Sally, who is also white, is much less likely to be pulled over when she's driving than Julio's wife, who is Hispanic. This seems like something that would upset the King of Rascals.

Jesus had to go through Samaria because there was something dreadfully wrong in the world.

He had to go through Samaria because he wanted to take a stand that would echo throughout the ages and say, "This is wrong."

There's something else the story of the Samarian woman tells us about the King of Rascals. The way he speaks with her tells that his attitude toward a person has nothing to do with gender and everything to do with the One who created that person. Imagine if the Bible, in John 3:16, said, "For God so loved males that he gave his only son." Or if in Ephesians 1:5 it said, "He destined those of us who are men to be adopted to be his sons." No. Adoption into God's family—salvation—is inclusive. Men and women stand side by side in the eyes of Jesus. When a culture pushes women down, Jesus has to go there and say, no, this is not right.

The Samaritan woman was flabbergasted that Jesus spoke to her. "How can you, a Jewish male, talk to me, a Samaritan woman?"

Throughout history, wherever Christ followers have gone, the status of women has been elevated and women have found freedom.

China is one example. For thousands of years, the Chinese had a practice of binding the feet of women. Have you seen pictures of this? Do a Google image search. It's quite shocking. Type in "China bound feet." It's really disgusting, and it happened because the men in that culture thought pretty little feet were cute and dainty and should fit in cute little shoes. You can see these shoes at the Natural History Museum in Chicago.

Full-grown women wore shoes just a few inches long. Because men thought this was attractive and they loved the tiny steps it forced women to take. When a little girl was only a few years old, they would wrap her feet incredibly tightly, and they stayed that way for her entire life. It was painful and it made a woman's feet deformed and so tiny and useless it was hard for a woman with her feet bound to even stand up. But these women were still expected to do all the housework and raise the kids. Can you imagine what that was like?

Foot binding is now outlawed in China. It was officially outlawed in 1911 by the Boxer government. Yet in rural areas the practice continued. The end of the practice in outlying areas had a lot to do with Gladys Aylward, a British Christ follower who became a missionary to China. For years she worked for this practice to end. She knew that this was not a practice that the King of Rascals would stand for! In 1932 the illegality of the practice was reaffirmed, in large part because of Gladys's efforts. Because of her efforts the law banning such a horrible practice was enforced throughout rural China.

Where the gospel goes, oppression is overcome.

Jesus does not like it when women are oppressed and in bondage. Gladys Aylward's campaign against foot binding helped change a cruel cultural practice and set women free.

The Samaritan woman? She was hosed. Five divorces and living with a dude who was not her husband. Good religious people of the day, and I dare say good religious people of our day, see such people and roll their eyes. We look down our noses and we say, "Well, they made their bed and they've got to lie in it." Stew in their own juices.

Religious people of that day, and religious people like you and me of our day, tend to see people who have issues and have made bad choices and get all hoity-toity. We like to look down our noses and shake our heads. But is that how Jesus sees it?

Mark, chapter 2, verses 16 and 17 tells about a time when teachers of the Jewish law spotted Jesus eating with people they knew were sinners and tax collectors. (Tax collectors were hated because they worked for the Romans and because they overcharged people and kept the extra money.) The teachers asked Jesus' disciples: "Why does he eat with tax collectors and sinners?"

Jesus overheard them and answered, "It is not the healthy who need a doctor, but the sick. I have not come to call the righteous, but sinners."

Jesus began a conversation with the Samaritan woman to let the world know that people who are messed up and sinful are the people he came to help. Jesus met her at the well at noon because he had to make a stand and say, "Messed up, rejected, filled-with-issues, sinful people are the reason I came."

Can we admit that we all have issues? If we can we will see the great news in this encounter between a rascal and the King of Rascals.

One of my favorite songs, by a group called Ten Shekel Shirt, begins this way: "Cheer up, you are worse off than you figure!" This is news we have to embrace, because we tend to think we are better than we really are. The bottom line is that we are rascals, prone to sin and to walk away from the Lord.

All of us have sinned.

All of us have got issues. We are not as hot as we sometimes think we are. We are as sinful as this woman at the well.

The good news is that Jesus came for each one of us anyway. We don't have to have our act together. We don't have to have it all in order. We don't have to be perfect. We don't have to be sinless. (And by the way, we can't be anyway, no matter how hard we try.)

The King of Rascals loves messed up people.

That hits me as good news, how about you?

I'm a rascal, a scalawag, prone to go my own way. I do things that the best part of me doesn't even want to do. In this way, I am just like the apostle Paul, who writes in Romans, chapter 7: "I don't do the good I want to do, and I do the evil I don't want to do." And I'd bet three dollars that you are a lot like me.

I'll bet you are a lot like that woman at the well.

So when we read that Jesus reached out to a woman who had issues and who'd been rejected by everyone around her, we ought to shout, "Praise God!" And remind ourselves, God has done that for us.

He came for us.

He had to come to earth, kind of like he had to go through Samaria.

In spite of our issues, in spite of our struggles—or maybe because of them—the King of Rascals comes to us in the midst of our shame and embarrassment and says, "Let's have a drink of water."

I like the King of Rascals. He's not angry, lightning bolt Jesus. He's not passive, distant Jesus. He's the King of Rascals who went through Samaria because there were people there with issues, people who needed his care.

Because he wants the world to understand that those are the people he came to help, he had to go through Samaria.

Chapter 4

Fig Tree Religion

Alright, let's review our purpose in this book.

We are taking time to fully understand who Jesus is as he's revealed in Scripture. We want to make sure we are totally clear about who this King of Rascals truly is. Then we will be able to choose either to accept or reject him based on who he really is, or to describe him to our friends who don't yet know the King of Rascals.

Let's look at what Jesus' disciple Mark says about Jesus in Mark, chapter 11, starting at verse 12.

> The next day as they [Jesus and his disciples] were leaving Bethany, Jesus was hungry. Seeing in the distance a fig tree in leaf, he went to find out if it had any fruit. When he reached it, he found nothing but leaves, because it was not the season for figs. Then he said to the tree, "May no one ever eat fruit from you again," and his disciples heard him say it.

Now jump down to verse 20.

> In the morning, as they went along, they [the disciples] saw the fig tree withered from the roots. Peter remembered and said to Jesus, "Rabbi, look! The fig tree you cursed has withered!"

What's going on? Has Jesus lost his marbles? He's talking to trees.

I had a seventh grade teacher who talked to plants in the classroom every day. She told us that talking to a tree or a plant would help it grow stronger and better.

Do you know what we thought of her?

We thought she was nuts!

And here's Jesus talking to a tree. And not only is he talking to a tree, he's not being very nice to the tree. I mean, c'mon Jesus, if you are going to be loony and talk to trees, at least be nice to them. "Oh, those are nice leaves you have." At least then (according to my seventh grade teacher) the trees would grow. But no, Jesus is grumpy to them.

Jesus is acting like a grumpy nut case.

We've gotta do some research, I think, to help us understand what is going on in this story.

Imagine you are walking down the street and you see a poster with a picture of an elephant painted red, white, and blue. When you see this, what do you think? Most astute Americans instantly think "Republican Party." We understand that elephant plus red, white, and blue equals Republican Party. We see it and think "Republican Party," and then a whole bunch of things that we connect with the Republican Party flow through our minds.

A red, white, and blue donkey probably will make you think of the Democrats. And when you see this symbol, you won't just think "donkey," or even just "Democrat." You also will think about all the things connected in your mind with the Democratic Party.

Now imagine you're looking at a photo of a fig tree. To someone in our culture, it's just a tree, right? But when a Jewish person of Jesus' time looked at a fig tree, that person thought about a lot more than just a tree. Just like we think about a lot more than just a certain kind of animal when we see a red, white, and blue donkey or elephant.

So instead of assuming that Jesus is nutty and grumpy, talking to trees, maybe we need to understand what a fig tree meant to people in the Jewish culture.

Do you know the first time fig trees are mentioned in the Scriptures? It's way back with Adam and Eve in Genesis, chapter 3. When Adam and Eve turned away from God, they realized they were naked. And they covered themselves with what? Fig leaves. Fig leaves are what Adam and Eve used to cover their shame. They had disobeyed God's command not to eat a certain tree's fruit, fruit that God assured them was deadly. The fig leaf was used to cover up their sin, and so it became a symbol in Jewish culture of the Jewish religious system. A system of laws that, if you obeyed them, could "cover" your sins.

If I were to show you a picture of a cross, you probably would instantly think of Christianity and all that goes with it. The Jewish people, when they saw a fig tree, would remember how fig leaves had covered sin and shame and disobedience.

They also would associate fig trees with abundant blessings from the Lord. In Deuteronomy, chapter 8, the Bible tells how God promised to bring his people, who had been freed from slavery after four hundred years, to a land flowing with milk and honey and filled with fig trees.

In Jesus' day, the fig tree was to the Jewish person what the cross is to a Christian person today.

So Jesus, seeing a fig tree in the distance, and being hungry, walked up to the tree and saw that there was nothing on it but leaves. He said, "May no one ever eat fruit from you again." The next morning as Jesus and the disciples walked along, they saw the fig tree had withered to its roots. Peter said to Jesus, "Rabbi, look! The fig tree you cursed has withered!" (Just to be clear, Jesus didn't swear at the tree. To say he cursed the tree means he passed judgment on the tree.)

But what Jesus was actually doing was making a huge, profound statement about the religious system in the place and time where he revealed himself as the son of God. He cursed that religious system, meaning he passed judgment on it. In "passing judgment" on the fruitless fig tree he was making a point about the fruitless system of the rules and regulations of the Jewish religion.

People who heard that Jesus had cursed the fig tree and who understood what Jesus meant would respond in one of two ways. People who were "professionals" in the religious system would be highly offended. He was saying, "This is not right." He was saying to the religious leaders of the day, "You only look good from a distance."

That's what the text says. From a distance, the fig tree looked really good, all green and leafy. And much of the religion of the Jews back then, and much of our religion today, quite frankly, looks good from a distance. So let's get out of their business and into ours.

A lot of what we do in American Christianity looks really nice from a distance.

We sing together. "Kumbaya, my Lord."

We hold hands.

We put a quarter or two in the bucket.

It looks great and people can look from a distance and say, "Wow, those are really good people."

But in cursing the fig tree that looked good from a distance but was fruitless up close, Jesus gets in the business of everyone who is involved in any religious system, like many of you and me.

Religion that just looks good leaves people hungry.

It's useless.

Like a fruitless fig tree.

That's pretty powerful, right? Religious systems that look good on the outside but do nothing to nourish the inner person are a waste of time and are worthy of the curse of the Lord.

Yikes.

I think that warrants some reflection on and examination of what we do by way of religious practice. Might be a good idea to take a time-out from reading and look deeply at your religious involvement. Is it life giving? Or does it only look good from a distance?

The King of Rascals cares much more about the impact than the appearance.

Let's round this out by looking at the rest of the story.

After Jesus cursed the fig tree, and before he and the disciples walked by that tree again the next day, the Scriptures tell us that Jesus went to the temple. This is one of the times we actually see Jesus get angry.

Very angry.

He's angry because the moneychangers and the people selling animals for sacrifice had, as Jesus says, turned his Father's house, the temple, into "a den of thieves." He makes a whip out of cords and chases the animal sellers and moneymen out of the temple, pushing over their money tables as he goes.

Holy smokes, had Jesus lost his mind?

No, he hadn't lost his mind. On the contrary he knew exactly what he was doing. Like his cursing of the fig tree, his outburst in the temple was another forceful declaration of how far off track the religious system had gotten. It looked good on the outside, but it was rotten on the inside. In fact the story of the fig tree is symbolic of what took place that day in the temple.

After this temple incident, the leaders of that religious system immediately began looking for a way to kill Jesus.

When you meet the King of Rascals, you can't be neutral about him.

He might make you really mad, angry, livid. He confronts people about what they're doing if it's not right. What he did and said made the religious leaders mad enough to kill him. The King of Rascals especially likes to confront people who are in positions of authority and power who are oppressing others.

That's why this angry Jesus is not the angry Jesus who's ready to blast someone who makes one mistake. The angry Jesus in our story is the Jesus who confronts people who oppress others using this thing called religion. That's worth getting angry about. A religious system that looks good from a distance but does nothing for people is worthless.

A lot of the people who hear that get mad. It ruffles their feathers.

But another group of people who heard what Jesus had done said, "Hurray!"

Hurray!

Praise God! Because the religious system represented by the fig tree had gotten messed up, and in turn it had messed them up.

When the King of Rascals confronted the system, the oppressed were set free. So while some people were angry with Jesus, others were tickled pink. (I don't know what it means to be tickled pink, but my grandma used to say it whenever something good happened.)

Jesus confronted the system that was killing people. Literally and figuratively.

God had given his people, the Jews, commandments to live by. God did this so people could see what rascals they were. God wanted people to see that no matter how many animals or coins they gave, no matter how many good works they did, they could never give enough, or pay enough, or do enough to cover up the fact that they were still rascals. And being rascals was keeping them from being able to have what God wanted for them, and what he meant for all people to have right from the beginning of time—a deep relationship, friendship, with God.

No matter how hard they tried, they just couldn't make it right with God.

And oh, how they tried.

And tried.

For the religious leaders of the day this reality became a source of power. For the commoner it became death.

When Jesus said, "The system's broken," many people—heavily burdened people—sat up and listened. And as they listened something stirred inside of them.

Hope stirred.

Maybe there was a way to get right with God.

Hope.

Have you ever tried to clean up your own act? In my experience, it doesn't work at all.

Have you ever done something that you know is not right, and said, "Man, that's not right. I am not going to do that again," only to find yourself a few days later doing the exact same thing again? And then how do you feel? You feel like an idiot. You say to yourself, "I am an idiot. I'm not going to do that again." You might even call a friend. "Hey, I am never going to do that again. Hold me accountable." And then you go away and you might be able to keep from doing it for maybe a month. But time goes by, and guess what? You are doing it again. The same thing, again.

Is this your story or just mine?

The Bible calls this eating vomit. "As a dog returns to its vomit, so fools repeat their folly" (Proverbs 26:11). Yuck.

It's the cycle of the stupid nature of humans, and when we are left to our own devices, we follow the "fig tree" religion that says it's up to you to save yourself and make yourself right before the Lord. Work harder. Obey the rules. Do this. Don't do that.

Let's be clear and let's be honest. If it's up to us we're all screwed.

When Jesus sees the fig tree and all that it represents, he says that this religious system is not the way to get right with God. As we've seen, that made some people angry and to others it was a great relief. But even if it was a relief, people would say, "Well, if that's not the way, tell us what the way is."

The apostle Paul speaks to this. In Ephesians, chapter 2, he says we are saved through grace.

Through God's free gift.

Not by anything we do on our own. Our fig leaves are no help at all. The reality is that we are all rascals; we all say and do and think awful things that make it impossible for us to be right with God. Each of us, like a sheep, has walked away, or run away, from the Shepherd. We have chosen to go our own way.

That is what makes us all rascals. And our rascally nature is what separates us from the love of God. And rascals left to themselves eventually wind up in some very bad places.

But the good news is that the King of Rascals loves all rascals and has the power to take away their rascallyness. So while it's true that if you have a pulse you have issues—that if you are human you struggle with sin—if you have the King of Rascals, your issues are covered and you are upright before God.

In 2 Corinthians chapter 5, verse 17, it says that if you belong to Christ you are a new creation; everything about you is new.

Trying to earn our way to God leads only to failure and shame. But when the King of Rascals adopts you as a son or daughter you become royalty yourself, living in God's kingdom.

Who knew?

So, fellow rascals, walk into the freedom of Jesus, the King of Rascals, and it will change your life. It will change the lives of the people in your life too. And you will live in God's kingdom.

Chapter 5

Geckos and Grace

His name is Bruchko. It's Bruchko because the natives of South America where he's a missionary can't pronounce Bruce Olson. In his autobiography Bruchko tells how one day when he was walking through the jungle from one village to the other, he sat down, leaned against a tree, and fell asleep. He dreamed a butterfly was trapped in his mouth and trying to get out.

It was a disturbing dream, but things got worse when he woke up. To his horror he discovered that it wasn't a butterfly but a tapeworm that was escaping through his mouth; it had been in his belly.

That's nasty.

To Olson, everything had looked good and felt good on the outside. He didn't know that there was something nasty going on inside. A tapeworm trying to get out.

Is that disgusting or what?

I once heard an urban legend about a woman in Arizona who went to a store and bought this cute little cactus. She put it in the sun by her kitchen sink. A few days after she had brought it home, she was doing dishes, admiring the cactus, only to notice that it was throbbing. So she called the place where she had bought this cactus and said, "Hey this cactus is throbbing; I didn't know cacti did this."

They told her, "Get that cactus out of your house right now!" She ran outside with the cactus and set it down in her driveway. No sooner had she put it down than it exploded with thousands of black widow spiders.

That may not be a true story, but it's still nasty!

When I was in fifth, sixth, and seventh grade, we lived on the island of Guam. My dad was in the air force. My mom was the social worker at the school I went to, and one of our Friday rituals was to stop at the bakery on the way home from school to buy pumpernickel bread.

Fresh pumpernickel bread from the bakery. It was awesome.

One Friday after we got home, my mom cut three slices off the loaf of pumpernickel—one for my brother Jason, one for me, and one for her. Mmmm, yummy. As my mom was chewing, we heard *crunch, crunch, crunch*. Not a sound your pumpernickel bread is supposed to make. Something hard was in the bread. She reached in her mouth and pulled out a foot of a gecko. True story! It turned out that a gecko, one of those small lizards that are everywhere in the tropics, had fallen into the loaf and got himself baked! My mom had chewed the foot of a gecko. I thought she was going to puke! The bread looked great on the outside, but it was nasty on the inside.

Now that you are thoroughly grossed out with tapeworms, spiders, and geckos, let's get to the Word of the Lord.

In the last chapter we saw the King of Rascals confront a system. In this chapter we'll see him confront an individual. The story about the rascal we are looking at now is found in Luke, chapter 18:

> A certain ruler asked [Jesus], "Good teacher, what must I do to inherit eternal life?"
>
> "Why do you call me good?" Jesus answered. "No one is good—except God alone. You know the commandments: 'You shall not commit adultery, you shall not murder, you shall not steal, you shall not give false testimony, honor your father and mother.'"
>
> "All these I have kept since I was a boy," he said.
>
> When Jesus heard this, he said to him, "You still lack one thing. Sell everything you have and give to the poor, and you will have treasure in heaven. Then come, follow me."
>
> When he heard this, he became very sad, because he was very wealthy.

If we don't understand what's going here we can run into a shallow misunderstanding of the text, i.e., that money in and of itself is evil.

In this passage of scripture, Jesus is saying something specific to a particular man, while at the same time upholding a larger principle. In upholding the larger principle the King of Rascals opens the door to address a host of practices associated with that principle.

Have you ever tried on one of those one-size-fits-all caps? We were in Orlando visiting my wife's parents, and since we were going to the Magic game that night I had to have a Magic hat. So I went to the store and bought this one-size-fits-all hat. Tried it on in the store; I looked good in it. I left the store and this hat was awesome, got in the car, and ten minutes later my ears were throbbing and my head was aching. What felt good at first didn't feel good at all a short time later.

So much for the notion that one size fits all. Our story about Jesus and the rich young man is not one-size-fits-all either. The story is not telling everyone, "Go sell your stuff."

This becomes clear in the very next encounter Jesus has. In Luke, chapter 19, Jesus meets another rich rascal, Zaccheus. But his encounter with Jesus ends very differently from that of the rich young man. When Zaccheus meets Jesus he immediately declares that he will give half of his money away to help the poor. What about the other half? Jesus does not tell him to sell all he has. Jesus' request for the rich young man to do so was obviously not a one-size-fits-all command.

There is something much deeper going on in this story than a one-size-fits-all application.

What do we know about the rich young ruler? The Greek word translated "ruler" is *archon*. This tells us that the rich young ruler was someone in a position of authority, an official or a religious, business, or political leader. A modern day equivalent would be a business owner, teacher, pastor, or lawyer.

The ruler asks, "Good teacher, what must I do to inherit eternal life?" We can't hear the guy's tone of voice when he asks this question, so we can't really be sure what his attitude is when he calls Jesus "good teacher."

How many of you had brown-nosers in class at school? Remember them? Just made you want to vomit, right? Always sucking up to the "good teacher."

After asking what he must do to be saved, the young man lists all the good things he has done. So maybe he was looking for Jesus' approval. Some people are always fishing for a compliment.

But it's also possible that the young ruler was simply a broken man. He had tried religion. He had tried doing good works. But he had come to realize that something was missing on the inside. So maybe he asked his question out of desperation and with humility.

Some of us ask the question with the attitude, "Jesus, tell us how good we are." Others, with a broken spirit, out of desperation, ask, "Lord, what do I do to inherit eternal life?" And some of us are one way on one day and the other way the next.

We can't be sure how the young ruler asked his question, but we do know it's the same question that many people are asking today. What do we do to get to heaven? What do we do to have eternal life? What do we do to have a grace-filled and peace-filled afterlife and not have to spend eternity away from God?

How do you think people in your neighborhood would react if you asked them, "Hey, how does someone get to heaven?" What do you think their responses would be? Do good stuff? Most folks think that getting to heaven is a matter of doing certain things, and doing them correctly: doing good things for people, obeying the Ten Commandments—and this is where the rich young ruler, our rascal, was coming from.

Now we can't be sure if he was arrogant or broken, but it does seem that he thought, "If I just do the right things, then I can get to heaven." Jesus says, "Nope." He says, "Nope, it's not about the things you've been doing since you were a kid."

Jesus messes with this guy's understanding of eternity. He looks at the man's inside reality, not his outside behavior. Jesus sees that this man has an issue of putting too much trust in money for his comfort and security, just like many of us do.

Jesus puts his finger on the man's heart and says, "Your issue is that you have made money your god. You crave money more than you crave me." The apostle Paul says, in First Timothy, chapter 6, verse 10, "For the love of money is a root of all kinds of evil." Not money itself, but the *love of* money. When the love that should be given to God is instead given to money, that's a problem. As Jesus himself says, "No one can serve two masters. Either you will hate the one and love the other, or you will be devoted to one and despise the other. You cannot serve both God and money" (Matthew, chapter 6).

And there is the larger principle. The King of Rascals wants to be first in our lives.

Not money.

Not achievement.

Not friendships.

Not even a spouse or children.

Jesus first.

Above all.

For our own benefit.

Jesus sees that this guy has an inside problem, a problem with his attitudes and priorities, not an outside problem with keeping up appearances and following the rules. Jesus is saying, "I don't care what your life looks like on the outside; you've got a tapeworm that needs to be taken care of."

He says, "Your cactus looks great but someday soon it's gonna explode with icky spiders; your bread looks tasty, but there's a dead gecko baked inside."

In short Jesus asks the young man to lay down the things that he craves more than he craves God.

And in saying this to the young man Jesus says to us, "It's not about your outward appearance, it's all about your inward reality. Lay down the things that you crave more than you crave me."

After the admonition to lay down such things, he says, "Come, follow me."

"Come, follow me."

In those three words, Jesus lays out the good news: to get eternal life, you don't have to go through a checklist of behaviors.

To walk into glory, when it's said and done, you don't have to do a, b, and c and then d, e, and f. You just have to follow the Savior.

"Come, follow me."

The story of the rich young ruler is not about money; it's all about the grace that Jesus offers. He's basically telling the dude, "You can't do anything to enter heaven on your own. The good news is, just follow me!"

The apostle Paul says, "If you confess with your mouth, 'Jesus is Lord,' and believe in your heart that God raised him from the dead, you will be saved" (Romans 10:9). Shocking to this rich ruler dude, and shocking to many who come at it the way he did.

I can just hear the guy saying, "Oh crap. I've worked so hard at doing the right thing." (I can hear him say that 'cause I've heard myself say it.)

Jesus says life is about much more than doing the right thing. The prophet Isaiah, in Isaiah, chapter 64, says all of the things we do on our own to try to be holy are like trash, like filthy rags.

The apostle Paul says, "Yes, everything else is worthless when compared with the infinite value of knowing Christ Jesus my Lord. For his sake I have discarded everything else, counting it all as garbage, so that I could gain Christ" (Philippians 3:8, NLT). The Greek word that is translated "garbage" is *skoupídia*. It's the Greek equivalent of "crap." All of my religious actions are crap if they are separated from Jesus. Relying on religious activity, obeying rules and regulations, just looking good on the outside, is like being a cactus filled with spiders. If we base our eternal life on what we do, we're hosed. And if that's what the young man in our story was doing, he was hosed.

It seems that deep down the young ruler knew that his actions left him short. It seems this way because he asked the question he did and because he loved money. I wonder if he loved money so much because it gave him some sort of affirmation that he didn't find in his religious activity. At least for a moment money provided some comfort and affirmation.

Or maybe it's something else for you.

I wonder what you love, like this dude loved money. I wonder if you love that thing to fill a void.

Hmmm…

Only the King of Rascals will fill that void.

It has to be like a huge weight taken off our shoulders when Jesus says, "Just follow me."

Because religious practice is oppressive.

And money is fleeting.

Then the Lord Jesus shows up and says, "You can't be holy by trying to follow all the rules. Just follow me. You won't find freedom in money."

Suddenly we are free from having to try to be perfect using our own power.

Now we can drop our burden of guilt and shame and stand up straight and tall. We can walk in Jesus' steps, follow him. It's so freeing to know that it isn't up to us to be perfect. We can never be perfect, but the good news is that we don't have to be.

We can set aside our clinging to money, success, fame, and all those other things that can't fill the emptiness inside. If we can set aside such things we can walk into the life-giving freedom that can only come through following Jesus.

Jesus came and said you don't have to be perfect to enter the kingdom of God, you simply have to follow him.

That's really good news!

Having a new life of joy and peace can never come by doing certain things in a certain way. It's not about being religious on the outside, it's about following Jesus and a change of heart on the inside. It's not something we can earn by doing good works or giving lots of money to a good cause. We can't ever do enough to be good enough to earn our way to God and live forever. What Jesus offers instead is grace—Jesus accepts us just the way we are.

And once we start to follow Jesus, our life starts to look good on the outside too. Once we have been changed on the inside by the grace of Jesus, once we have been saved by grace through faith and not as a result of good works, our outside will look pretty sweet as well. As we follow Jesus, as we become more and more like him, loving others and doing good just naturally begin to flow from our lives.

So, you rascal, quit trying to be religious; quit working hard to look good on the outside. Keeping up appearances while you're dying on the inside is not what it's about. Just quit trying. Follow Jesus.

Let go of those things that you crave more than Jesus. They are shallow and won't last. Follow the King.

Because getting to heaven isn't up to you. It's up to the one who simply says, "Come, follow me." It's about grace.

Chapter 6

The Stinky Gate and the Pool of Slim Chance

Jerusalem in Jesus' time was surrounded by walls, like a fortress. To get into the city you needed to go through one of many city gates. The Sheep Gate was one of those gates. It was called the Sheep Gate because sheep and lambs used in sacrifices in the Jewish temple were brought through that gate. Thus the name Sheep Gate. Very creative. Sort of like the Dutch folks who named the first Reformed church in a town First Reformed Church and the second Reformed church in a town Second Reformed Church and so on. Creative. Like Sheep Gate.

The Jewish people's worship traditions often included slaughtering sheep. When they gathered for worship they would bring a sheep up front, slit its throat so the blood would spill all over, and then chop the sheep up into many pieces and offer it to God. Through the prophets in Old Testament times, God had told the people of Israel, the Jews, that the broken, bloody body of a sheep had to be offered to the Lord as payment for the people's sins.

The Jewish people knew that their sin separated them from God and that it took a broken, bloody body in order for them to be right with God. So for the Jews of Jesus' time, the Sheep Gate was a symbol of salvation through this act of sacrifice and slaughter. It was a powerful symbol of the hope and forgiveness that God had promised would one day be fulfilled in the Messiah, a deliverer who would be sent from God and who would set them free from sin and death once and for all.

Of course the Sheep Gate also was a place of death and, according to the history books, a place that smelled really bad.

Have you ever gone by a slaughterhouse on a hot afternoon?

Stinky.

The Sheep Gate was not a place where you would set up a family picnic. It was a place of death, a place of horror, and for sheep it was kind of like Hotel California. They could check in but could never leave. They went in and then they would die.

Across the way from the Sheep Gate, within sight of it, was a pool that was called Bethesda.

John, chapter 5, says:

> Jesus went up to Jerusalem for one of the Jewish festivals. Now there is in Jerusalem near the Sheep Gate a pool, which in Aramaic is called Bethesda.

The literal translation of the Aramaic word Bethesda is "house of mercy." The custom or tradition associated with the pool of Bethesda was that every now and then an angel of the Lord would come down and stir up its waters, and the first person into the pool would be healed from whatever ailed them.

So right across from the pool called House of Mercy, a place of hope and restoration, is the Sheep Gate, a place of the religious establishment, a stinky place of death. Verse 3 says:

> Here [between the place of hope and mercy and the place of stinky death] a great number of disabled people used to lie—the blind, the lame, the paralyzed.

Have you have ever watched the Christmas TV program *Rudolph the Red-Nosed Reindeer*? Rudolph, because of his shiny nose, becomes a social outcast, runs away, finds peace with himself, and by the end of the story, becomes a hero and gets the girl—or if you want to be technical, the doe.

In the course of his adventures, Rudolph visits the Island of Misfit Toys. While Rudolph is there we, the viewers, are introduced to many memorable characters. There is Charlie-in-the-Box—poor fella wasn't named Jack. Then you've got Bird Fish, a toy bird who swims instead of flies; a misfit cowboy who rides an ostrich; Trainer, a train with square wheels on its caboose; and that gun that squirts jelly instead of water. We look at the Island of Misfit Toys and we say, "Oh, that's cute."

But if you are Charlie-in-the-Box, who was set aside and ignored because he was named Charlie instead of Jack, the Island of Misfit Toys becomes a living hell.

At the pool of Bethesda, the place filled with people who were lame, paralyzed, blind, or deaf, we basically have a large group of misfits, people who did not belong in the regular society of their time. Like the toys in *Rudolph* they were set aside, cast aside; they had no place. It was a real life island of misfits—and there was nothing cute about it.

These misfits hung out in this no-man's-land, between a place of hope and mercy and a place of death, hoping they would be first to get into the water on a day when an angel would stir up the pool.

Can you imagine the deep longing of those people who were fighting to get into the pool first? They lay right outside the Sheep Gate, the place where sacrifices were made, but those sacrifices did nothing to bring them healing. And just once in a great while the pool might offer them a way to be whole again.

Have you ever been there? Stuck, sitting in your brokenness, and wondering where to go for healing and help? You try the religious way—you try to follow the religious rules, behave a certain way, act a certain way—and while your life looks better on the outside for a while, inside you still feel empty and hopeless. Once in a while you see someone else who is broken get set free from their brokenness, but with no one to help you move toward the pool of mercy and hope, after a while you just resign yourself to being stuck where you are.

One man lying by the Pool of Bethesda had been an invalid for thirty-eight years.

Wow.

Thirty-eight years.

People back then, and people today, might look at someone like him and say, "What did he do to get there?" Maybe you've heard something similar.

This is your fault.

You need to try harder, and maybe if you work harder, offer more sacrifices, you will be set free.

Just roll in the pool when it gets stirred. What is your problem?

Pull yourself up by your bootstraps.

Clearly there is something wrong in your life. You are messed up. If you have an addiction you are an idiot.

If you are a sinful person stuck in your sin, what is your problem?

Work harder.

Strive harder. Make it happen!

Or maybe you have made such statements, either out loud or in your head, about folks who are struggling. Be warned. Often people who say such things to the people lying in no-man's-land sooner or later find themselves broken and lying between the pool of mercy and the place of death, wondering how they got there.

Verse 6 says, "When Jesus saw him lying there and learned that he had been in this condition for a long time, he asked him, 'Do you want to get well?'"

There is beauty in that verse.

Maybe the most beautiful thing is the fact that Jesus was right there with the people who were in a living hell.

Being stuck in brokenness, shame, and rejection is hell, and Jesus is there. Jesus does not avoid unpleasant places. He will not leave us on our own in tough places. He comes to us and says, "I am here to do something about it."

This is good news.

The King of Rascals does not leave us on our own in our hell and brokenness. If you have suffered loss of any kind, abuse of any kind, shame of any kind, Jesus says, "I am with you."

"Do you want to get well?" Jesus asks the man. This is awesome. Jesus stands between the pool and the Sheep Gate. Between the place with hope for mercy, and the place of bloody sacrifice.

Do you know what John the Baptist called Jesus? He called him the Lamb of God who takes away the sins of the world. And this Lamb of God shows up outside the Sheep Gate, the place where sheep are led to the slaughter to cover the sins of the Jewish people but a place that has done nothing for the brokenness of these people. The Lamb of God shows up beside the pool of Bethesda, where people are healed once in a blue moon.

The King of Rascals brings together in himself the death and the sacrifice of the Sheep Gate and the hope and mercy of the Pool of Bethesda. He is the Lamb of God who has come to live among us and to save and heal the whole world.

When Jesus encounters the man who had been waiting for healing for thirty-eight years, he says to him, "Do you want to get well?" Now, you may be thinking, duh, Jesus. Of course the man wants to get well. He has been lying there for thirty-eight years! Why would you even ask that question?

If you have ever been stuck in your junk and your sin and your addiction, you know why Jesus asked the question. To put it bluntly, people *like* their junk and their sin and their addictions. If addictions weren't enjoyable people wouldn't be addicted! If your sin wasn't fun you wouldn't prefer to wallow in it. If the pull of darkness wasn't strong, you wouldn't be pulled there over and over again. When Jesus asks, "Do you want to be well?" he is asking, "Do you truly want to be free? Do you really want to have wholeness in your life?"

This is a crucial moment for the guy. In many ways, it might have been easier for the dude to say, "No. For thirty-eight years I have been doing life this way, and I have found a way to survive and cope."

You can see how that might be comfortable for him, in a distorted way. To be healed would mean he would have to give up begging, his current way of making a living. To be healed would mean his world would be turned upside down; everything would be different and strange.

"Do you want to be well?" See, it's a gentleman's question that Jesus asks, because when the King of Rascals shows up in the life of a person as the Lamb of God who takes away the sins of the world, he will mess that person's life up.

I'm thinking of Jesus' mother, Mary. An angel came to her with a message from God saying, "You're going to give birth to the Savior," and her life was turned upside down. When the Lord comes, life is turned upside down. So he asks the question. He won't force himself on anyone.

Do you want to be well? Do you want to have your life turned upside down, changed into something entirely different?

Do you truly want to be well?

It's an empowering question, not an enabling question.

Verse 7 says:

> "Sir," the invalid replied, "I have no one to help me into the pool when the water is stirred. While I am trying to get in, someone else goes down ahead of me."

Now I wonder if the guy said this in a whiny voice, kinda like I would sometimes when I am stuck in my own junk. Woe is me, life is really tough. Of course I *want* to get well but I just can't. You don't understand the pressures I face, you just don't understand...

I wonder if that's you too. I wonder if you are like what I imagine this dude to be. You fall into self pity. "I can't change. Oh, I have tried, but somebody else always gets the blessing instead of me."

Is this what Jesus does with the man at the pool? "Awwww, buddy, I am so sorry." No. Jesus confronts the man and doesn't allow him to sink into self pity, because with self pity the focus is on us, and when our focus is on us, guess what? We are stuck, going nowhere. Jesus calls him out of his self pity to look at the Lamb of God who takes away the sins of the world and has something to offer him that no religious system or fortunate circumstances can ever offer—healing and life.

Lift up your chin, shake off self pity, and look to the One who will change your life. His name is Jesus. Jesus said to the man, "Get up!" Get up! Jesus doesn't shame the man or condemn him, but instead

The Stinky Gate and the Pool of Slim Chance

there's a sense of "quit wallowing in your crap and get up!"

Get up! Hey, do you want to get well? Then get up! Get up! Pick up your mat and walk! Get up!

St. Augustine once said, "Pray as though everything depended on God. Work as though everything depended on you."

Think about that for a moment.

Jesus didn't let the man sit in his self pity. Jesus says, "Okay, then get up!" Move! Take action, an act of faith, an act of obedience. If you want to be free, walk in obedience and faith—get up and pick up your mat and walk.

And does the text say that in about three hours the guy got feeling in his toes and then in another two weeks he felt a little tingling in his left knee? What does it say? What are the next two words? AT ONCE! Now! Bam! Get up and walk! Boom! He's on his feet:

> At once the man was cured; he picked up his mat and walked.

Unbelievable! Thirty-eight years of being an invalid. Then one encounter with Jesus, and the power of God came on him and he got up at once. When Jesus encountered people on the earth he brought the power of the kingdom of God, and that which was not right was made right.

At once.

Let's talk about Jesus and healing for a moment.

Jesus says in John, chapter 14, "Anyone who believes in me will do greater things than I have done." Read that again, because it is shocking. Jesus has just cured a man who had been sick for thirty-eight years. At once. And a few chapters later, he says, "If you believe in me you will do greater things that I have done." Wow.

In Matthew, chapter 10, Jesus says to his disciples, "I give you authority to cast out demons and cure every sickness." In our rational, logical Western mindset, this is shocking to us. But if we had grown up in a developing country, the power of God would not be a shock to us. It would be a normal way of living. Stories abound of the miraculous taking place in developing countries. Blind people see, lame people walk, deaf people hear—because in those countries they don't have the "Enlightenment" approach to understanding God that pushes the reality of the power of Jesus back two thousand years.

The King of Rascals came in power and then gave that power to his followers. Jesus' people today, wherever they go, bring the power as Jesus did when he walked on the earth.

When my oldest son, Jake, was twelve and in seventh grade, he played football. At practice one day, I watched as Jake and one of his friends took part in a drill where guys line up in a three-point stance. The coach blows a whistle and the players run at each other and smack into each other and knock each other down.

Jake's friend led with his head. He's a big kid, and he hit another big kid full-speed in the chest. That dude went straight down, his arms stiff as he fell. Boom! He lay there unconscious. It was incredibly scary as the coach, on his knees beside the young man, screamed his name. *"Stay with me! Stay with me!"*

We all thought this kid was going to die. An ambulance came, immobilized him, carted him off to the hospital stiff as a board, wrapped up and unable to move. Jake and I went that night to see him in the hospital. He was laying there with a neck brace on, unsure about how he was, as the doctors hadn't examined him yet. He was waiting for an MRI, and he couldn't move all that much. I said, "We are going to pray for you."

So Jake and I prayed for this kid.

The hospital let him go home the next afternoon.

Was that because of our prayers, because we prayed in the name of Jesus who brings such power that lame people get up and walk? We'll never know for sure. But Jake and I prayed and we took that power that Jesus evidenced in the story of the man healed at the pool of Bethesda to a hospital in Kalamazoo.

Or what about my knees? After three ACL tears and four reconstructive surgeries the doctors told me to take up knitting. I was only thirty-two.

The church gathered around me to pray at one of our mid-week services.

And nothing happened.

They prayed again the next week.

And nothing happened.

In the spirit of the persistent widow, they prayed again for me the third week.

And my knees were healed.

I play hoops every week. I run several miles each week. I've even run a marathon and several half marathons. All after I was told I would never be active again.

Or what about Dave, who had hepatitis C until we prayed for him?

What about the Smiths, who were unable to conceive until we prayed for them? They have four kids now.

What about Aaron, who had epilepsy, until we prayed for him?

Could it be that Jesus actually meant what he asked for when he prayed for the kingdom of God to come to earth?

I'll bet the man at the pool would answer that question with a resounding "Yes!"

This is the King of Rascals. The King of sick rascals.

This is the Jesus who encountered a man who had been lame; this is the Jesus who bridges the hope of religion and the hope of healing and brings them together in himself, the Lamb of God who takes away the sins of the world. This is the Jesus who comes with power to heal.

This is the King of Rascals.

Not only does he heal, he gives us the power and authority to heal.

For Jesus, it seems that healing people was as normal as breathing. But for us it seems shocking because we aren't used to it as part of our everyday living. If you are sick, if you're not well physically, wouldn't it be awesome to encounter this healing power of Jesus?!

For years I suffered from insomnia. I was on Ambien. It's a freaky drug. I'd pop a pill at night and go to bed. In the morning I'd wake up, go to the gym to work out, and later in the day couldn't remember that I'd gone to the gym. I would touch my clothes and they were sweaty. Yeah, I was there, but I don't remember going. That's not right. So I had people pray for me, and now I sleep like a baby. I'm not an insomniac anymore.

Matt struggled with depression and was on antidepressants. He had some Christ followers pray for him. He doesn't struggle with depression any more.

Jane had strep throat the week before a huge, much anticipated vacation. Not good. She asked some folks to pray for her. She went on vacation healthy as a horse.

If you are like the man at the pool, stuck in physical pain, find people who will pray with you. The man at the pool was healed, and at once he picked up his mat and walked.

Here's a wrinkle in the story. The day on which Jesus healed this man was the Sabbath, the day when, according to Jewish law, Jews were supposed to do no work whatsoever. So the Jews said to the man who had been healed, "It's the Sabbath. The law forbids you to carry your mat." They see a miracle—a man who has been an invalid for thirty-eight years is now walking—and they say to him, "It's the Sabbath! What do you think you are doing carrying that mat?"

The Jewish religious leaders had taken God's command not to work on the Sabbath to extremes that God never intended. They were accusing this guy of sinning by picking up the mat he had used to lay on next to the pool.

Do you think that maybe while they were zeroing in on this supposed breaking of the law they actually missed what was really important? Their reaction is a perfect example of what happens when we run to the Sheep Gate—when we cling to the do's and don'ts of religion and miss the freedom and healing God has for us.

Trying to be holy by following religion's rules and regulations always brings death and never celebrates life. Religious practice that is done just for the sake of following the rules always brings shame and guilt. It can never celebrate the life that comes to a person through a relationship with Jesus.

This seems to be a common theme as we look at Jesus' interaction with rascals.

We see instantly that these religious guys are just idiotic. The dude was just healed and they are worried about carrying a mat on the Sabbath?!

Yet if we are honest, we too are probably guilty of caring about things that really don't matter.

Your music is too loud.

Your clothing isn't right.

She smokes!

He didn't raise his hands like he should have during worship.

She raised her hands during worship.

That person waved a flag in worship.

This person didn't wave a flag in worship.

None of these things matter! What matters is that someone's life that was broken is now whole because that person encountered Jesus.

When we cling so hard to religious rules and regulations that we miss the reality of what God is actually *doing*, that's just stupid and leads to death.

So what does that mean for you? I'm thinking you probably don't want to be like the folks who saw the man who encountered the miraculous and say, "Hmmm, you are carrying your mat, shame on you."

When we see life where there once was death, that is worth celebrating. These dudes should have been like, "Wow, give me some of that.

You got healed! Way to go! We celebrate with you! You were broken and now you're whole. You were lost and now you're found!" But they didn't, they just got all snooty.

What a pity.

In verse 11, the man who was healed tells the Jews, "The man who made me well said to me, 'Pick up your mat and walk.'" So they asked him, "Who is this fellow who told you to pick it up and walk?" The man who was healed had no idea, because Jesus had disappeared into the crowd.

Later, Jesus found the guy at the temple and said to him, "See, you are well again. Stop sinning or something worse may happen to you."

What?! That is as clear as mud, isn't it? I mean, is this grumpy old Jesus again?

Here's what's going on. Jesus comes to set us free. He comes with his power and does miraculous things, but he doesn't do those things as an end in themselves. The miracles are to draw us closer to Jesus, so that we might walk in communion and intimacy with him.

Jesus rebuked the man because he had cried out to Jesus, received the power of Jesus, and then went his own way, not even bothering to figure out who had healed him. We do the same thing. We want God to bless us—"Bless me, give me what I need. I am down on my luck, God. I need your help today!"

How many of us have cried out to the Lord in a time of great need and had our prayer answered? If we only call on God when we need something but never get to know the One who has answered our prayers, we've missed the whole point.

Jesus will say, "Hey knucklehead, it's not just about the power. It's about who I am, and I want to be in relationship with you."

The King of Rascals came for relationship.

The keys to that relationship are daily interactions with the Lord through reading his Word, through prayers that go beyond asking for stuff. If we don't enter into a relationship with Jesus, become intimately connected with him, we've missed the whole point.

At The River, the congregation I serve, intimacy with Jesus is our highest value. Because everything else—love, joy, peace, patience, godliness—flows out of that intimacy. We don't want people to be religious, we want them to know Jesus, to interact with him regularly.

Coming to church on Sunday is a good step in that direction, but it is not the whole story. If Sunday morning is the sum total of our time with Jesus, at some point we'll begin to feel empty and dry and have a hard time living a life that honors God. Get into the Word. Find a Bible reading plan for the New Testament. Pray when you feel like it and when you don't. Get to know Jesus and the life he offers you.

Try praying, "Lord, would you teach me how to pray?" Or ask someone who prays all the time to teach you how to pray. Attend a prayer study group to get trained and equipped.

The world needs a lot of prayer, so you need to grow in intimacy with Jesus. Don't just take from him; walk in relationship with him. Jesus is the Lamb of God. The Sheep Gate sheep were a sign pointing to the real thing.

The King of Rascals is the real thing.

Jesus allowed his body to be broken because God says that where there is sin, there needs to be a dead and broken lamb. Jesus took the nails, the thorns, the whips. He allowed himself to be broken so that the sins of the world would be covered by his blood.

His body was broken and his blood was spilled, but there was a crucial difference between this Lamb and every other lamb that went through the Sheep Gate. The Sheep Gate wasn't the Hotel California for Jesus. He checked in, but boy did he check out! God raised Jesus, his son, to life again. The tomb they laid Jesus' body in is empty.

And because his body was broken and his blood was shed, our sins are covered. When we say yes to Jesus, to becoming his follower and friend, Jesus delivers us from the kingdom of darkness and gives us the gift of life.

Do you want to get well?

Chapter 7

Canaanites and Aristotle

> Leaving that place, Jesus withdrew to the region of Tyre and Sidon. A Canaanite woman from that vicinity came to him, crying out, "Lord, Son of David, have mercy on me! My daughter is demon-possessed and suffering terribly." Jesus did not answer a word. So his disciples came to him and urged him, "Send her away, for she keeps crying out after us." He answered, "I was sent only to the lost sheep of Israel." The woman came and knelt before him. "Lord, help me!" she said. He replied, "It is not right to take the children's bread and toss it to the dogs." "Yes it is, Lord," she said. "Even the dogs eat the crumbs that fall from their master's table." Then Jesus said to her, "Woman, you have great faith! Your request is granted." And her daughter was healed at that moment.
>
> Matthew 15:21-28

"It is not right to take the children's bread and toss it to the dogs"? Jesus called the Canaanite woman a dog! The King of Rascals has gone grumpy again. What's up with grumpy Jesus? Maybe Jesus is just having a bad day.

To figure out what's going on here, I did what I often do. I went to the ancient language. I have this dictionary of old Greek words that translates them into our English. So I looked up the word "dog" in the Greek language of the New Testament. The Greeks had lots of words for dog, just like we do: puppy, pooch, hound. The word Jesus chose to use when he called this woman a dog is the word for little dog or puppy.

So I thought, well, maybe that gets grumpy Jesus off the hook. Maybe he's using a term of endearment, like, "Awwww…you little puppy. Come here, you little puppy, and give me a hug." So maybe he's not grumpy Jesus; maybe we're just missing something in the translation.

But then I was talking to a pastor friend of mine. I asked him about this text, and he reminded me that this woman whom Jesus called a dog came from Canaan, from the same place that Queen Jezebel came from.

And this would have been of great significance for the Jews who were with Jesus that day, and all Jews of Jesus' time. Centuries earlier, Queen Jezebel was a Canaanite woman who had married a king of Israel, King Ahab. She became the most evil, vile, nasty woman in Israelite history.

Back in Jezebel's day a prophet had declared that someday her blood would be licked up by dogs, and sure enough, the prophecy came true. Jezebel was thrown from the walls of the city of Jerusalem, and she splattered all over on the ground and the dogs licked her blood.

For Israelites, any woman from Canaan was bound to be evil. My pastor friend clued me in that Jesus is not calling the Canaanite woman a little puppy; he is calling her a dog, exactly what all Jews knew that Canaanites were.

I said, "Oh crud. Grumpy Jesus is still on the hook."

How do we figure out this text? How do we understand what's going on between the major players in this story? What is going on between the Jews and the Canaanites?

In answering these questions, we learn something helpful about the King of Rascals.

The Canaanites were the oldest enemy the Israelites had. After that whole Adam and Eve thing, the Lord spoke to a man called Abraham and said, "Leave your land." The Lord told Abraham to leave his land and go to a new land, and guess where that new land was? Starts with a "C" and ends with an "anaan." Canaan.

Long, long ago, the Lord told Abraham and his people to go and live in Canaan, the land of the Canaanites (obviously). The descendants of Abraham, the Israelites, have been in conflict with the Canaanites ever since.

Throughout Old Testament history, whenever the Canaanites enter the story they are enemies of the Israelites. The Israelites and the Canaanites never get along. So when Jesus calls this woman a dog, he's referencing three or four thousand years of tension between Jews and Canaanites.

Canaanites represented all that Jewish people despised. The Jewish people believed in one God and in separating themselves and following that God. The Canaanite religion, on the other hand, allowed everything and anything: idol worship, child sacrifice, all sorts of weird sexual practices in their temples. They despised the way of the Jews.

The two groups hated each other.

And while God had called the Jews to be separate from people who were idol worshipers, they took that call to be separate and turned it into something God never intended—they turned it into elitism.

True, to follow God the Jews needed to separate themselves from the people around them. This was good. But the Jews turned this separateness into elitism: everyone else was wrong and less than them. An Israelite in Jesus' day would naturally think, "No matter what others do, what we Jews have is never going to be theirs. It has nothing to do with them. They are nothing but dogs."

Well, bummer! Doesn't get grumpy Jesus off the hook, does it? What is Jesus doing when he calls this woman a dog?

Have we finally found an unappealing flaw in the King of Rascals' character?

Did you notice that when she called out to him, he ignored her? He didn't even address her until the disciples said something.

And then he said the exact same thing that any Jewish person of that time would have said. The common, accepted, racist practice was to spurn and look down on all Canaanites. Jesus was saying the same thing any elitist Jew would have said.

So it seems like it's not bad enough that he's grumpy Jesus; seems like he's elitist, racist Jesus.

But before we draw a final conclusion let's take a look at something I learned from Aristotle. I had to read a book by him when I was taking a post-graduate class at seminary. The book was titled *On Rhetoric*, and it was written thousands of years ago.

Rhetoric is the art of communicating. I remembered something I learned from that book, and a light bulb went on in my head in connection with our story.

Aristotle's book teaches people how to communicate in ways that engage other people, ways that get people's attention. (Ironically, Aristotle, this great teacher of the art of communicating, wrote the most god-awful boring book on communication I have ever read in my entire life.) One important rule that Aristotle teaches is that people must get the point you are trying to make.

According to Aristotle there are many ways, many rhetorical devices, that communicators use to make a point. Voice inflection—changing how loud or soft you speak and your tone of voice—is one technique that speakers use to make a point. Have you ever had a preacher or teacher speak in one tone the whole time, never changing the tone of their voice? It's a real snoozer, isn't it?

Hyperbole. Hyperbole is exaggerating something to make a point. Like, "I have a *ton* of laundry to do." Have you ever said something like that? It's a way to get someone's attention.

And then of course there's the..........dramatic pause.

Now throw in direct eye contact and you have another tool of engagement for public speaking.

Speakers use lots of ways to get people's attention.

Another rhetorical device is using reverse psychology. As I was looking at this story about the Canaanite woman and remembering Aristotle, I realized I recently had used reverse psychology to make a point.

I was making a presentation at a church just up the road from The River in a town called Zeeland. Zeeland is home to Vriesland Reformed Church, a church that's been around for over a hundred years. The pastor is a friend of mine, and he has a vision from the Lord to lead Vriesland Reformed in planting a new church.

My friend realizes that Vriesland Reformed, like many churches, tends to be a bit nervous around the topic of church planting. Yet, he wants them to look outside their own walls and begin to minister in their community. And he believes that the best way for them to do that would be to plant another church. He knew that the folks at Vriesland Reformed were highly opposed to starting a new church. Since I am a church planter who works with church planters, he asked me to come to Zeeland to speak to the congregation.

So the first thing I said when started to speak to the folks at Vriesland Reformed, with my pastor friend sitting right there, I said, "I'm wondering if you're wondering, *Is this man crazy?* He is crazy. He's nuts! I mean, aren't you wondering if he's nuts?"

And everyone's saying, "Yeah, I think he's nuts."

I said, "Isn't he crazy to ask me to persuade you to plant a church? Do you know how expensive it is? I think he's crazy, don't you?"

The whole crowd is mumbling. "He is crazy."

I told them how it took two hundred thousand dollars when the church I lead, The River, planted a new church called Vanguard. I told them about the emotional cost as well. We miss the members of our congregation who left to go plant Vanguard.

"Is he crazy?"

"Yeah, he's crazy."

I had them.

I said, "But do you know what? He's walking with the Lord, because Jesus is about a movement that changes lives and not about a monument that keeps us sitting in the pews."

I had presented their arguments like they were my own and then, boom, I began to take them down scripturally one by one. In the end, many in the church were saying, "We've got to plant a church today! We gotta do it!"

They were ready to move because they could see that their reasons for not planting another church were blown away by what God says about the real reason churches exist—to change lives.

So back to the Canaanite woman whose daughter is possessed by demons. She walks up to a bunch of Jews, Jesus and his disciples, and says, "I need help. My daughter is possessed."

And Jesus turns his back on her. "I was sent only to the lost sheep of Israel."

And the disciples must have said, "That's right, Jesus, you ignore her. She's one of those Canaanites. Send her away, Jesus. She keeps hollering after us. Send her away! That's right, Jesus, you were sent for the Israelites alone. Let's exclude all of those people, get rid of them!"

The woman comes and kneels in front of Jesus. "Lord, help me!" she cries.

Jesus replies, "It is not right to take the children's bread and toss it to the dogs."

"Yes it is, Lord," she says. "Even the dogs eat the crumbs that fall from their master's table."

The disciples chime in again. "That's right, Jesus! That's a dog over there; she doesn't deserve what we get. The mercy and grace and love of the Father are for us Jewish people. We got it going on. It's not for those Canaanites, and she's one of them. *Get outta here, dog.*"

And then what does Jesus do?

Bam! He's got them. Bam! He takes the disciples' stupid, sinful, human, elitist, God's-mercy-is-just-about-our-group attitude, and he says, "No!"

He confronts their wrong attitude by showing them exactly what they look like, and then he turns to the woman to say, "You have great faith! Your daughter is well!"

So what Jesus is doing here is confronting a system of oppression and injustice that has to end. He is saying, "There's a new way of understanding in town. God's mercy is not just for the few, the proud, the social or racial elite; it isn't just about us Jews. It's about every person who comes to me. *Every* person who comes to me will be saved."

Jesus says "No!" to that stupid thinking that looks at another person and says:

> He is a dog.
>
> He is not as worthy as we are.
>
> She doesn't deserve what we've got.
>
> We have the grace of God. They don't.
>
> We have God's mercy, and it's not for them. Get them out of here!

Jesus says, "Woman, you have great faith and your daughter is well."

All who come to Jesus will be saved. All who call on the name of the Lord will be saved.

God did not send his son into the world to condemn the world.

God sent his son for whom?

All.

For God so loved the world that he gave his one and only son that anyone, anyone, not a small group, anyone who believes in him will be saved.

All.

But, but, but…Jesus? You suckered me there. She's from Canaan, Jesus. Her people messed with Abraham. Her people messed with the Israelites and King Ahab. Before she can have anything to do with you, don't you have to tell her to act right, behave right, dress right, do church right, and all that stuff?

She just came straight to Jesus! And that was enough for him to say, "That's great faith."

You simply come to Jesus. That's the faith he's looking for. He's not looking for people to get all the behaviors and rules right first. You just come to Jesus exactly as you are and you will find life, just like the Canaanite woman and her daughter.

The King of Rascals came to turn religious systems that are exclusive upside down and show people a God whose arms are open wide, who loves you and says, "Just come to me."

What's ironic and sad is the fact that the disciples themselves knew what it was to be rejects. They were rascals themselves. Having received the friendship and grace of the King they should have been willing and ready to dole it out to another rascal. But they weren't.

Some of us rascals have been called dogs for too long. Some of us have felt like outsiders because others have said, "Send her away. She's a dog." So it's good news to learn that there are no dogs in the presence of Jesus. Just people that he loves.

Others of us have a tendency, like the disciples, to keep a wall between certain rascals and us. We choose to be gracious to this type of person and that type of person, but not to those people who don't measure up to our standards. Keep those folks over there, please. Send them away.

So to myself and to you, I say, "Stop it."

Just stop it!

The woman came to Jesus with baggage, loaded with Canaanite paganism. But she came to Jesus, and she found life. And an affirmation of her faith.

Here's the point: Jesus is the point.

Some of you have got really crappy lives. Maybe you're unemployed. Some of you have got marriages that just stink. Some of you just don't enjoy life.

Follow the lead of the pagan Canaanite woman who simply came to Jesus and said, "I need help."

Let the King of Rascals give you life.

Chapter 8

Lewis's Logic

Does the name Marshall Applewhite mean anything to you?

Back in the '90s, this dude thought that there was a spaceship behind the Hale-Bopp Comet that was passing near Earth. He claimed, "I am Jesus." He believed that as the Messiah, he was to lead his people onto this spaceship hiding behind the comet and they would enter into Glory.

There was one hitch.

To get onto the comet spaceship and into Glory, his followers had to kill themselves.

In March 1997 Applewhite committed suicide with thirty-nine of his followers in Rancho Santa Fe, California. They mixed phenobarbital with applesauce or pudding, then washed it down with vodka. Then they placed plastic bags around their heads in case the drug didn't kill them.

What do you think about Applewhite claiming to be the Messiah? Do you: A) believe he is the Messiah, or B) believe he was a nut job?

Probably B.

What would you think if I said, "Well, yeah, I don't think his claim to be the Messiah is true. He probably was a nut case. But you know what, he was a really good teacher."

What would you say to me? You'd shake your head and say, "No, anybody who thinks there's a spaceship behind a comet and we have to kill ourselves to get to it is just not right in the head. He can't possibly be a good teacher."

Or how about Jim Jones? Does his name ring a bell? Back in the '70s he was quoted as saying, "I am Buddha and Jesus reincarnated." Wow. I mean that's like me saying I'm Shaq and Jordan rolled into one. A pretty heavy claim.

Jones also claimed to be the Messiah. He claimed to be the hope of the world who would take people into Glory, into the Promised Land. He convinced 909 of his followers that the way to get there was to drink a grape-flavored drink laced with poison. It was the largest mass suicide known to humanity.

Do you believe: A) Jim Jones' claim to be the Messiah is true, or B) he was a nut-case and full of dooky?

I agree with you. But what if I said to you, "You know what, I know he was wacky and I know he led 909 people to kill themselves, but he was a great teacher."

Would you buy that? You might say, "Well, he was influential man, but I'm sure he wasn't a great teacher."

Way back in the 1800s, Arnold Potter told people, "I am the Messiah, the Potter Christ." He was a little more creative in his Messiah complex: the Potter Christ. In front of his followers, he rode a donkey to the edge of a cliff, and then stepped off the cliff that he might ascend into heaven. Much to the dismay of his followers, and most likely himself, he descended rapidly and died a rather sudden death.

Do you believe Potter's claim to be the Messiah? No. Nut job, full of dooky. But was he nonetheless a great man and a great teacher? No.

David Koresh. The year was 1993. He led the Branch Davidians down in Waco, Texas. He claimed, "I am the Lamb of God." And he fathered fifteen children with girls as young as twelve. Do you believe his claim to be the Messiah? Do you believe that he was maybe a nut job and full of dooky? Yeah. And certainly not a great man or a great teacher.

It's time for the rubber to hit the road. I want to lay out for you, incredibly clearly, the claims that Jesus made about himself and that one or two of his closest followers made about him.

I want to be totally clear: Jesus believed wholeheartedly that he was the Lamb of God, that he was the Messiah.

When Jesus was hauled before the religious leaders a short while before he was crucified, the Jewish high priest asked him, "Are you the Christ, the Messiah, the Son of the Blessed One?" And Mark 14:62 records Jesus' response. Jesus said, "I am."

In the gospel of Luke, chapter 4, Jesus is in the temple, and he stands up and reads this passage from the Old Testament book of Isaiah: "The Spirit of the Lord is on me, because he has anointed me to proclaim good news to the poor. He has sent me to proclaim freedom for the prisoners and recovery of sight for the blind, to set the oppressed free, to proclaim the year of the Lord's favor" (Luke 4:18-19).

"Today," Jesus adds, "this scripture is fulfilled in your hearing."

He had just read a prophecy that was a thousand years old and that told of the Messiah, the savior of Israel, who would come one day. Religious folks had been waiting for thousands of years for that prophecy to come true.

Jesus was saying, "I am the one the prophecy is about." He believed that he was the Messiah.

In Luke, chapter 5, when Jesus is speaking to a man who is paralyzed, he says to him, "Friend, your sins are forgiven." The religious leaders were appalled. "Who can forgive sins but God alone?" they said. By saying to the man, "Your sins are forgiven," Jesus had claimed to be God.

Is he really another Jim Jones? Another Arnold Potter?

"In the beginning was the Word," says John, speaking of Jesus, "and the Word was with God, and the Word was God. Through him all things were made; without him nothing was made…in him was life, and that life was the light of all mankind" (John 1:1, 3-4).

Also in the first chapter of the gospel of John, in verse 14, it says, "The Word became flesh and made his dwelling among us."

Who is the Word? "Word" is referring to Jesus. Jesus, according to John, was there at the creation of the universe and existed before the beginning. In fact, he has always been and all things were created through him. Jesus is God. Jesus is the Messiah.

In John, chapter 8, verse 46, Jesus says, as he's being questioned by the religious leaders, "Can any of you prove me guilty of sin? If I am telling the truth, why don't you believe me?"

Jesus claims to be the Messiah, to be God, to be present at the beginning of time, and to be sinless.

These are audacious claims.

And in John, chapter 10, verse 28, he says, "I give them [my followers] eternal life, and they shall never perish."

Jesus is making some large claims—those who follow him will have eternal life and will never die.

And one more. Jesus says, "I am the way." I am *the* way. He does not say, "I am *a* way." The word translated here is "the," spelled T-H-E. "I'm THE way and THE truth and THE life. No one comes to the Father except through me."

Now, Jesus, Marshall Applewhite, Jim Jones, Arnold Potter, and David Koresh all have something in common. All five of these dudes claimed to be the Messiah who would lead people into the Promised Land.

Many people look at Jesus and they see a man who was respectable and a great teacher. And many say about Jesus, "Well, I don't think he was the Son of God, but he was a good man and a great teacher."

In fact, many world religions regard Jesus as a great teacher and a great man. Let's name a few: Hinduism, Buddhism, Judaism, Islam. And not just world religions, right? Many agnostics, kind of irreligious people, they sorta like Jesus, because he's kinda cool. I mean, when you look at Jesus you can't help but like him. But that claim to be the Messiah, we don't like that. We'll just say Jesus was a great man and a great teacher.

And many within the family of Christianity, people who claim to believe Jesus is who he says he is, certainly do not live like they truly believe he is the Lord of lords and King of kings.

On one hand we have Jesus, who says he's the Messiah. On the other hand are all these folks who say, "Nah. But he is a great teacher."

Lewis's Logic

So who's right?

Both sides can't be right.

We have to choose.

C.S. Lewis, one of the great theologians and fiction writers of the twentieth century,* had something to say about this rejection of Jesus' claims to be the Messiah while still holding him up as a great teacher.

Lewis was a professor of medieval theology and literature at Oxford and Cambridge. And many of his fellow professors would say, "I see Jesus as a good man and a great teacher but I do not believe him to be the savior of humanity, the Messiah."

Lewis called that "patronizing nonsense":

> I am trying here to prevent anyone saying the really foolish thing that people often say about Him: I'm ready to accept Jesus as a great moral teacher, but I don't accept his claim to be God. That is the one thing we must not say. A man who was merely a man and said the sort of things Jesus said would not be a great moral teacher. He would either be a lunatic—on the level with the man who says he is a poached egg—or else he would be the Devil of Hell. You must make your choice. Either this man was, and is, the Son of God, or else a madman or something worse. You can shut him up for a fool, you can spit at him and kill him as a demon or you can fall at his feet and call him Lord and God, but let us not come with any patronizing nonsense about his being a great human teacher. He has not left that open to us. He did not intend to.
>
> C.S. Lewis, *Mere Christianity*

Them's fighting words.

Lewis lays out what has become famously known as his "trilemma"— the argument that logically it's simply not possible to say that Jesus is

---

*You might be familiar with his Chronicles of Narnia books, which have been made into movies recently. If you view these movies with some understanding about Jesus and the Bible, you will pick up on strong biblical themes in them.

a great man but not the Messiah. As Lewis points out, there are only three options for us when we look at Jesus in light of all the claims he made about himself.

First of all, maybe Jesus is a nut job. Maybe he's just a lunatic, the word that Lewis uses. Maybe he's simply crazy. His claims to be the Messiah are like a madman's claims to be a poached egg. Maybe he is crazy, because clearly claiming to be the Messiah is way outside the norm. So one logical conclusion is that Jesus is a lunatic.

Second option, Jesus is simply a liar. He knew deep down he was not the Messiah, deep down he knew he wasn't who he said he was, but he lied and deceived everyone. And, Lewis argues, if someone intentionally deceives humanity and leads them down a path that he knows is untrue, he cannot possibly be considered a great man and a great teacher. Such a man is a liar from the pit of hell. He's a fraud, another Jim Jones or Marshall Applewhite or David Koresh.

As Lewis points out, there is only one other option: Jesus is who he says he is. Jesus really is the King of kings, the Lion of Judah, the Lamb of God sent by God to take away the sins of the world. The King of Rascals.

There are only three options when it comes to believing who Jesus is: 1) he's not in his right mind, in which case he can't be considered a great teacher, 2) he's a liar, in which case he's certainly not a great man, or 3) he is who he says he is, the Messiah, in which case he's a lot more than a great teacher. He's the Son of God, who came to offer the whole human race the way to be free of sin and death and to live forever with God.

Jesus is either a lunatic, a liar, or the Lord.

Here's the deal. We've spent some time getting to know the King of Rascals.

We've seen his interactions with the underdog.

We've watched him take on the religious establishment.

We've seen him heal the sick and the lame.

We've seen him confront oppression.

Lewis's Logic

We've seen him bring life where there was death.

We've seen that he really loves rascals.

Now you have a choice to make. I'm talking specifically to those of you who don't yet know Jesus as Messiah, as Lord. You need to make up your mind about who Jesus is, and then either reject him or accept him. As Lewis points out, Jesus never intended for us to have any other option.

You might not be ready to make a decision today. But if you've decided that you like what you've learned about Jesus, and you've decided you'd like to follow him, I invite you to find a group of Christ followers and make it public that you believe Jesus is who he says he is. They will welcome you as a sister or brother and help you to grow in Christ, to become more and more like Jesus, which is the whole point.

Do you want that? Do you want to walk in relationship with the Lord, the King of Rascals?

And what about you people who've claimed Jesus as Lord for a long time? People like me, people who have a pulse and therefore have issues. People who have the tendency to lean into rascalhood—to say Jesus is Lord with our mouths but to say otherwise with our actions.

With our mouths we say, "Yeah, I believe Jesus is Lord," but with our time, talent, and treasure we choose our own way over his.

Today is a good day to re-surrender your life to the King of Rascals.

Rascals to Royalty Part 2

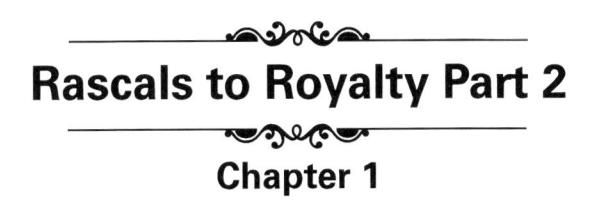

Chapter 1

No More Kate the Commoner

We've learned that a rascal is a rogue, a scalawag, prone to mischief. And that according to the apostle Paul, all have sinned and fallen short of the glory of God. We've learned that according to the prophet Isaiah in the Old Testament all of us like sheep have gone astray, each of us has gone our own way.

We've learned that we are a bunch of rascals.

We've also learned that Jesus, the King of Rascals, does not dismiss rascals as the world around him was prone to do. We've seen that he liberated the rascals he came in contact with and set them on higher ground.

Now, in this second section, I want to announce the dawn of a new era.

The King of Rascals is still the King, but the rascals are rascals no more.

That's right! The rascals are rascals no more!

Does the name Kate Middleton mean anything to you? She married Prince William, second in line to the English throne, who may someday be king of England.

Someday she may be queen.

When they got engaged people were shocked and outraged. One news writer said, and I quote, "He's supposed to marry one of his own."

Kate Middleton was just a commoner! Again I am quoting: "He could have married any woman in the world, but he chose Kate the commoner." Shocking! That this man of royalty would marry this common woman named Kate, whose mother was a flight attendant and whose father was a pilot who became a businessman. (He owns a mail-order party favor business, and the big joke was, "Well, maybe they will give them a discount on favors for the wedding.")

She's now going to be royalty.

She will live a life of privilege that she could only have dreamed about when she was younger.

That life of privilege began when Prince William proposed and gave her a ring with an 18-carat sapphire surrounded by fourteen diamonds. That thing was so big she practically had to wear a sling to show it off.

Now that she's married to him she has her own private secretary. What do you do with a private secretary?

She is no longer Kate the commoner, she is Lady Kate, a royal duchess.

She has her own bodyguards.

Top fashion designers beg her to wear their clothes, because anything that Duchess Kate wears instantly becomes popular.

How would you like that?

If she wanted to, she could live in a palace.

She will never have to worry about money again.

Nor will she ever have to worry about cleaning the house—er, I mean palace.

She had a $40 million wedding, and it's estimated that over three billion people watched her get married.

She started off with nothing.

Wow. Talk about a dream come true.

From commoner to royalty.

Now the news analysts managed to say one good thing about her, even though they were shocked she was a commoner. They praised her wisdom because "she was prepared to wait on the crown."

See, Kate and William dated for eight years. I mean, come on dude, just pop the question already.

Eight years she waited.

But she understood that this wasn't an ordinary courtship. She wasn't marrying Joe Schmo, she was marrying into royalty, into something bigger than her and beyond her.

She was prepared to wait.

Let the crown be first.

She could take second.

So they praised her for her wisdom in doing such things. Way to go, Kate!

It's a great story, isn't it?

Well, quite frankly, her story is our story. We are commoners chosen to become royalty. As we look at what it means to move from being rascals to being royalty, the Bible verse on which we will hang our hats for this chapter and the next three chapters is 1 Peter 2:9.

> But you are a chosen people, a royal priesthood, a holy nation, God's special possession, that you may declare the praises of him who called you out of darkness into his wonderful light.

Peter calls Christ's followers "a chosen people, a royal priesthood." The parallel between Kate Middleton's story and our own is uncanny. We were commoners, rascals, who were chosen by the King to become royalty.

Peter says back in 1 Peter, chapter 1, verse 1, that the words he is writing are for "God's elect, exiles scattered throughout the provinces of Pontus, Galatia, Cappadocia, Asia and Bithynia." These are the people he is calling "chosen," "royal." The fact is, these people had been rejected by their society; they couldn't even call their home "home" because people thought they were so weird that they persecuted them and kicked them out of their homes. These early Christians had to scatter and flee.

To the society of their time, these people were nothings, nobodies, the kind of people that others would point at and say, "You are a rascal, a rogue, a scoundrel, a scalawag; you have nothing to offer. Be gone with your bad self."

But they are also the people that Peter, inspired by the Holy Spirit, calls "royal."

Kind of cool for them, isn't it?

It's too bad that what was true for them isn't true for us today, right? I mean, wouldn't it be nice if we too could say that we are royal?

Maybe we've made really bad choices or have been rejected by others, and we feel worthless and embarrassed.

We know what it means to feel like a second class citizen who lives in the shame heaped on us by others and by ourselves.

Isn't it a bummer that we can't be royal like those early Christ followers?

Remember when I talked about rhetorical devices, things communicators use to help people pay attention and remember what they're talking about? The previous statements are just a way to get your attention.

Because the truth is, what was true in Peter's time is true today. Christ's followers are rascals who have become royalty.

Think about what a rascal and a knucklehead you are.

How many of you have treated someone you love dearly very poorly in the past month?

How many of you have been upset with yourself because you have gotten angry yet again, or you did that thing you said you would never do again, or you went back to that addiction you never wanted to go back to?

The really good news is that Jesus does not look at us and say, "You are a rascal." Instead he says, "You are a chosen people, called to be royalty."

That's great news, isn't it?

Maybe you don't realize what a rascal you are. That apart from Jesus you're just an idiot. And maybe you don't realize that you are prone to go your own way like a stupid sheep. Maybe you don't understand that all of us are like sheep. (Sheep are used as an image of Christ followers in lots of places in the Bible.)

Did you know that when a sheep falls over on its back, it can't get up on its own? Have you ever seen this on the Discovery Channel? If upside down sheep are left on their own, they will die of starvation and thirst. This image perfectly captures us in our rascalhood.

A disservice has been done to some of us who grew up attending church. Because we've walked in the grace of this King of Rascals, we tend to forget that we come from rascalhood. We tend to take being a chosen people—chosen by the King of kings to be a royal priesthood—for granted. And this is a disservice to us. A disservice we do unto ourselves.

It's like we're saying, "So what? I have a brown hoodie on today and I am wearing black shoes and I am chosen; I belong to a royal priesthood, now what's for lunch?"

We need to grasp the reality that we once were really knuckleheaded rascals who've become royalty because the King has chosen us to be so.

Go look in a mirror. Point at yourself and say, "You're a rascal, a rogue, a scoundrel, a scalawag. You are prone to wander and prone to mischief. But in Jesus, you are a new you. In Jesus, you have been chosen to be one of his people, and you've been called to belong to a royal priesthood."

So what does that mean?

That's what we'll look into in the next few chapters, but let me give you a little teaser.

It means that you are new. It means that you are no longer defined by your common status.

You are no longer Kate the commoner.

You are Lady Kate, a royal duchess.

The Word of God calls you the bride of Christ. You've married into royalty and therefore you are royal yourself. The life you used to live is dead and gone. The life you live today is new because of what Jesus has done for you.

It means, praise God, that if you are following Jesus you will have life in heaven when you get there. Who wants to go to hell? Anyone? The beauty of Christ is that there is eternal life with God after death.

But that's just part of it. The beauty is also that we get new life here on earth. We don't have to wait to die to experience the joys of Jesus. Because we are royalty we have royal blessings that we can walk into here on earth. We'll get into that in more detail in the next chapter.

And because we are royalty, we do not have to be afraid to approach God. How many of you are little scared of God? Is that just me sometimes? How many of you are a little scared and intimidated? When I was little, I used to think God was huge and distant, big and scary, and I had to crawl up to him and beg on my knees.

But because we are chosen people, a royal priesthood, the Bible tells us that we no longer have to approach God in timidity. The Bible says we can approach the throne of grace with boldness. We can go boldly before the King of kings, the Lord of lords, the creator of the universe, and talk to God in our prayers like we would talk to a friend.

Jesus says, "I no longer call you servants...I have called you friends" (John 15:15). Our prayer life can be drastically different. We don't have to grovel and grope before the King. We can stand up and say, "I am royal, too, and Jesus, I need help in this and this and this. Jesus, will you help me?" And because we are royal in status, the Bible says whatever we ask for in Jesus' name here on earth will be given to us.

Have you been scared to try that one out? More on that later.

I just want to make sure that you know that I am not making this up. You are a chosen people.

A holy nation.

A royal priesthood.

So what else does that mean?

Victory.

Don't you love it? Are you a basketball or football fan? Don't you get excited when your team wins? Victory is good.

Because we are a chosen people, a royal priesthood, we can live a life of victory.

The days when the sins of our life beat us up again and again can be behind us if we walk in a royal status as the chosen people of God. Victory is good.

Kate Middleton was considered incredibly wise because she waited on the prince's timing. It took eight years before she got that fifty-pound ring on her finger, but because she waited even nasty newscasters applauded her for her wisdom.

You, as a chosen people, a royal priesthood, do what she did, and remember to put the King first and yourself second. When we walk that way, the benefits are unbelievable. We'll continue to unpack the benefits of being royalty.

For now, remember one thing. You are one of God's chosen and royal people. So begin living like it.

Welcome to royalty, you rascal.

Chapter 2

This Is Jericho

Let's go to Jericho. Do you remember who fought the battle of Jericho? Joshua fought the battle of Jericho.

Jericho in Joshua's day, more than 3,400 years ago, was a place of abundance. It was in the land that the book of Deuteronomy describes as flowing with olive oil and honey. In fact the name Jericho literally means "fragrant."

It was an appealing place. Jericho was called "The City of Palms" because there was an overabundance of palm trees. With an average temperature of 75 degrees and constant sun it was the ancient equivalent of West Palm Beach, Florida. Everybody wanted to go there.

Jericho had many springs, so water was plentiful even though there was barely any rainfall. People grew lots of crops by irrigating the land. Jericho is still such a great place to live that it's the oldest continual settlement on the face of the earth. People have lived in Jericho since the beginning of time because of the richness and goodness of the land.

To the Jewish people, Jericho represented God's promise of abundant, blessed living for his people. When God brought the Jews out of slavery in Egypt, he promised them a land of their own. The Lord said, "I will give you this land." And in giving the Jews this land, the Lord promised that when his people walked with him, they would walk in abundance and joy.

Jericho symbolized that abundance and joy. To the Jews, who had been wandering in the desert for forty years after leaving Egypt, the Lord said, "You are going to cross over the Jordan River and you are going to enter into the promised land."

The first place they encountered in the promised land was Jericho, this land of abundance.

Unfortunately, that's not the only thing it was. Deuteronomy, chapter 9, verses 1 and 2, says: "Hear, Israel. You are now about to cross the Jordan to go in and dispossess nations greater and stronger than you, with large cities that have walls up to the sky. The people are strong and tall..."

So it was a place of abundance that symbolized the promises and blessings of the Lord, but it was also a place where the Israelites were going to meet strong opposition. The people in the promised land were bigger and stronger than the Israelites and the walls of the cities in the promised land reached the sky. Archaeologists tell us that the walls of the city were a little over fifty feet tall. They stood on a steep embankment, which added another twelve feet to the wall.

So we see that at times there are things that block and deny God's people access to God's promise of abundance. To the Jewish people back then the walls of Jericho represented obstacles to receiving the abundance God had promised.

The story of Jericho is told in Joshua, chapter 6, beginning in verses 1 and 2,

> Now the gates of Jericho were securely barred because of the Israelites. No one went out and no one came in. Then the Lord said to Joshua, "See, I have delivered Jericho into your hands, along with its king and its fighting men."

That's good news, right? The Lord says, "I know there is opposition to the promise I have made to you, but I am going to deliver it to you." Verse 3 tells what God instructs the Jews to do so that Jericho will be theirs:

> March around the city once with all the armed men. Do this for six days.

Yeah! Now that is some military strategy. Here is how you will take the land. Just march around it once a day for six days. I don't know what the fuss was about in Afghanistan. We should have just walked around it. Did we really need all that demolition back in Iraq with Saddam Hussein? We could have just walked around it, right? Makes perfect military sense.

Well, no. But then God gives further instructions in verse 4.

> Have seven priests carry trumpets of rams' horns in front of the ark [of the covenant]. On the seventh day, march around the city seven times, with the priests blowing the trumpets.

Now it makes more sense, right?

> When you hear them sound a long blast on the trumpets, have the whole army give a loud shout; then the wall of the city will collapse and the army will go up, everyone straight in.

Amen. Military strategy at its finest! So Jericho symbolizes the abundance and promise of the Lord, the opposition to God's people to get to that abundance and promise, and a God who is high on crack.

So what happened? Starting with verse 15, it says:

> On the seventh day, [the Israelites] got up at daybreak and marched around the city seven times in the same manner, except that on that day they circled the city seven times. The seventh time around, when the priests sounded the trumpet blast, Joshua commanded the army, "Shout! For the Lord has given you the city!"

And in verse 20:

> When the trumpets sounded, the army shouted, and at the sound of the trumpet, when the men gave a loud shout, the wall collapsed; so everyone charged straight in, and they took the city.

I guess God wasn't on crack after all.

Jericho not only symbolizes the abundance that the Lord has for his people and the opposition that stands before God's people. It also represents, and maybe this is the point, the shocking and amazing victory to be had for people who follow the Lord.

When we become Christ followers, when we move from rascals to royalty in Christ, when we listen to God and obey God, God gives us amazing victory, victory against all odds, the ability to overcome the obstacles set in our way to get to abundance and the promised land that he has for us.

The victory that God gave the Israelites over Jericho is amazing in two ways. First of all, the way God asked them to go about it is just nutty. I mean, no one writing the history of Israel would even think about making up something like this. Who would imagine this way of getting victory? All the marching and the horn-blowing and the shouting is just a nutty way to do it.

So what does this tell us?

Maybe we've got to do some nutty things to get through the opposition, to get through to the promised land that the Lord has for us.

Hmmm…maybe you've got some dots that you need to connect. I can't connect them for you, I can just lay out the principle.

The Israelites' victory over Jericho is a shocking victory. I can imagine the people saying to the Lord, "I don't think you get it, God. Give us a catapult and then we will take 'em. Give us big swords and then we will take 'em. Give us a tank a few millennia early and then we will take 'em. We don't want to walk around the city. So we're just going to sit here, Lord, until you give us something to work with, something that looks a whole lot better."

What victory would they have had? None. Theirs is a shocking victory because it required nutty things of the people. And without their walk of obedience, there would have been no victory.

Did you catch that? Without their walk of obedience there would have been no victory.

That is still true today. The Lord has promised us a life of abundance and blessing. And we run into opposition when we move into that life. But that opposition will fall in the face of the Lord.

Sometimes the people who oppose us are bigger than we are; sometimes the walls that are in the way reach to the sky. But as Scripture says, "[B]e assured today that the Lord your God is the one who goes across ahead of you like a devouring fire. He will destroy them; he will subdue them before you" (Deuteronomy 9:3).

We see that it was God who brought the victory over Jericho. All the people had to do was walk in obedience.

What walk of obedience do you have to take? This is your homework. You've gotta figure this out. What walk of obedience do you have to take? Get off your butt and start walking where God wants you to go. If you don't do the walking, you will have no victory and no abundance of blessings.

The Israelites' victory is shocking because it was a victory where none was expected.

It had been forty years since God had first promised the Israelites they were going into the promised land. Way back then, the Lord had brought the Israelites out of Egypt after they had spent four hundred years as slaves to the Egyptians. The Lord led them as they traveled across a wide wilderness and right up to the land God was going to give them.

The Israelites sent twelve spies ahead of them to check out the land. Ten of the spies looked at the tall, strong people and the city of Jericho and they reported back, "The people in that land are bigger than us, stronger than us, and their walls reach to the sky! Ain't no way we're gonna do it."

Two of the spies said, "God is with us; we can do this."

But of course the people listened to the ten naysayers.

So God said, "Okay, since you are chicken and not willing to trust me, we are going to delay your entry into the promised land for forty years."

So by the time of Joshua, the people had been exiled, set apart from the abundance of the Lord and without victory, for four hundred and forty years!

That's a long time.

I don't know long you feel like you have been stuck in your junk. It hasn't been for four hundred and forty years.

Although it sure might feel like four hundred and forty years.

Now really, think about that. 'Cuz lots of us have some junk in the room. And it feels like the wall in front of us reaches to the sky. And it feels like the way things are has lasted forever and will never change.

It's important for us to remember that when the Israelites took that walk of obedience, the wall that seemed insurmountable and the separation from God's blessings that had lasted forever fell, and they had victory.

This is the lesson of Jericho.

This is the blessing that we get when we walk with the King who brings us from rascalhood to royalty.

You are no longer a rascal; you are a royal priest, a chosen person, a member of God's holy nation. You can have victory. Just like the Israelites at Jericho.

Let's take a look at a New Testament story that's set in Jericho. Remember Zacchaeus? He's the short fellow who climbed a tree so he could see Jesus. He was a tax collector and hated and despised by his people. Tax collectors stole out of the pockets of their own people, stabbed them in the back for their own selfish gain. In Jesus' day, if anyone seemed beyond the grace of God it was tax collectors.

Who are the tax collectors of our day? Who would you name? Who is so evil and wicked that they belong on the other side of the wall?

Zacchaeus had heard of Jesus and was drawn to Jesus at the very core of his being. So he did everything he could just to get a glimpse of the one who became King of kings and Lord of lords.

Jesus looked up and saw this man who was desperate to see him, so desperate that he would set aside his dignity and climb a tree. And he said, "Zacchaeus, I am coming to your house today."

And when he did, Zacchaeus became a Christ follower.

Radically transformed.

He told Jesus he would give half his possessions to the poor and pay back four times what he had taken from anyone he had cheated.

The story of Zacchaeus is a Jericho story with a twist. It's still the story of abundance blocked and then, boom, victory for someone who could not have had victory doing things according to his own plan.

The story of Zacchaeus teaches us that when we encounter the King, the walls will go down and abundance comes in even when everyone else says, "No, you deserve to be on the other side of the wall."

Jericho is not mentioned much in the New Testament, maybe five or six times, but when it is, Jericho is a place of victory. Another example is the story of a blind beggar named Bartimaeus in Mark, chapter 10. He had been blind for decades, living in squalor, in poverty, in need and want. Definitely a huge wall between him and victory. But when Jesus came by, he screamed for Jesus, and people told him to shut up. "Don't interrupt the rabbi, he's important." Jesus said, "No, I am here for him because he needs to be on the other side of that wall." Bang! Guess who received his sight? The walls of Jericho came down all over again.

Throughout the New Testament, wherever Jericho pops up the story is about people who were walled off, blocked from abundance from the Lord, and who then experienced victory when people thought victory was not a possibility.

Sounds like a great place, this Jericho.

The reality is that for people chosen by God victory is inevitable. Abundance will be theirs. It is simply a matter of God's timing and our obedience. But victory is ours. The walls of Jericho will come down.

We need to have right understanding of who we are. We are sinful people who have been saved by grace! Sometimes we act like rascals, but that does not define us. We are people who are saved by the grace of the Lord and are now a chosen people, a royal priesthood, a holy nation, a people who can walk in victory.

Are you tired of living a defeated life? Are you tired of old junk haunting you? Are you tired of not seeing change? Well, I say Jericho to you! The truths of the Old Testament that we see in the New Testament are true for us today.

The apostle Paul says in Romans 8:37, "[I]n all these things we are more than conquerors through him who loved us."

As royal people, we can choose to walk in victory. We don't have to settle for a life of ho-hum. We can walk as victorious people because of Jericho and the God behind Jericho.

But it's a choice we have to make.

Remember the twelve spies that went into the land? They saw people who were bigger and stronger and they said, "It's kind of safe right here where we are."

Some of us look at our junk and say, "Wow, that is insurmountable. I don't want to do the hard work to get at that."

Sometimes it is hard work to walk toward our freedom.

Sometimes it seems safer where we are, even without the freedom. At least it's comfortable and familiar.

But two of the spies, Joshua and Caleb, said, "No way, God is bigger than this."

I recommend going the way of Joshua and Caleb and walking into victory.

My friend Doug Mc Clintic is a pastor who planted a church in California. The Lord gave him the vision to start a new church. God showed Doug that he was behind the vision in a couple of ways. One way was through what Doug read in the Word, the Bible, and the other way was through a couple of people Doug trusted. These people were already doing the new church thing, you know, reaching out to people who don't like the traditional church. These people said to Doug, "The Lord is going to bless your family as you plant this new church."

So Doug and some others started the new church, and the day the church was scheduled to open its doors to the public, Doug's ten-year-old son, who is autistic, got up at two in the morning and—it's hard to find a delicate way to describe what he did—had a bodily function in his bed and smeared it on the walls.

That night it took Doug an hour and a half to clean the textured walls in his son's room.

The same thing happened every night for the next three months. This was no laughing matter.

Doug will tell you, it was draining and taxing, and he wished he would have remembered that there is victory to be had. He and his wife, in the midst of this gunk, could barely manage to get up every morning...they were just drained.

But some of their godly friends heard about what was happening, and they came over to the Mc Clintics' home one night and prayed for blessings and abundance.

They basically prayed Jericho over Doug's son. They prayed the blessings of Jericho: that the walls would come down, and that the family would be blessed, that the son's behavior would end.

Just one night of prayer, and the kid never ever did it again.

This is the kind of victory that the Lord has for us and that we have to get to. Sometimes we have to be reminded that God will give us victory. We just need to move forward, with God's direction, to go through the walls, the obstacles, to get there.

Another man I know, an angry man, was an alcoholic, spent years in jail. He would do all the things he needed to do to get clean, but he found himself in jail again and again and again.

But then, he told me, one day he met Jesus. He said, "I want people to meet Jesus because it radically changed my life. I am no longer angry. I no longer desire alcohol. I am a free man because I met Jesus." Jericho is real today.

A friend of mine was counseling a guy who had left his wife years before. While the guy was in the counseling relationship, the counselor said to him, "Why don't you come to church with me?" So the guy went to church with his counselor and met Jesus. Well, the guy told his ex-wife that he was now going to church. And she thought, "Well, maybe I'll go to church." She started going to the same church.

Guess who have remarried and now have a marriage like they never had before?

This is Jericho. In the here and now.

One Sunday at The River, we had people stand up for healing, for physical healing with back and leg problems. Later that day, I got a text from a dude who had had back pain for all kinds of years. A long time. We prayed for his back that morning, and guess who has no back pain?

This is Jericho coming into our reality. When we walk into royalty and leave our rascalhood behind, we join a people who are victorious.

Stand tall. Hold your head up high. Be victorious!

Chapter 3

Her Royal Highness

Black and white, when they are together, are sharper and crisper.

Sweet and sour, when they are together, mmmmm…it's so tasty.

Contrast is how we are going to get at this next lesson.

Let's begin in April 2009. Barack and Michelle Obama took a trip to meet the Queen of England for the first time. On their way to visit the queen, the Obamas were given a list of rules of etiquette and how you conduct yourself in the presence of royalty. Here are a few items on the long list of things they had to comply with.

When approaching the queen, never reach your hand out to her and certainly do not touch her unless she first extends her hand toward you. And if she extends her hand toward you, count yourself fortunate, for she rarely shakes hands.

If she extended her hand, the Obamas were allowed to reach out and clasp, but not grip, the queen's hand, and certainly not shake it. You do not shake the queen's hand. You hold it lightly, mildly, in that fish-hand thing that makes us all want to vomit. You hold her hand really loosely so that when she pulls away you can back away.

All this hand-shaking etiquette was just rule number one on how to behave in the presence of royalty. You've got to know your place and act appropriately.

The second thing the Obamas had to learn was what to do with their hands at other times. You have two options in the presence of royalty. You can clasp your hands in front of you or you can clasp them behind you. Never put your hands in your pockets in front of the queen.

And of course, the third thing, they had to learn how to curtsy, at least Michelle Obama did. And Barack had to learn how to bow appropriately. Because in the presence of royalty you need to know your place and you need to know how to honor that which is royal.

And it's expected, when you're visiting the queen, that you bring a gift. The Obamas brought a video iPod, etched with some really nice words on the back and encased in silver. On the video iPod were Barack Obama's inauguration speech and a video of the Queen of England's visit to America a few years ago, along with special music that the Obamas arranged to have composed by the queen's favorite artist. Pretty cool.

The queen gave the Obamas a picture of herself. It wasn't even signed. (When it came to the gifts, the Obamas got screwed.)

The last thing the Obamas had to learn about how to behave in the presence of royalty was that if you have the unbelievable fortune of having tea with the Queen, you must not gulp your tea. You may not slurp your tea. No slurping, please! You have to sip your tea. And you can't hold the saucer. The saucer must be on your plate. You sip your tea, and you put your cup down between each sip. Because you gotta know your place in the presence of royalty.

There is something about us humans that naturally wants to be subservient to that which we think is bigger and better than us. And there is something in us that wants others to be subservient to us when we think we are bigger and better than they are, especially when someone is the queen of England.

Have you ever met someone famous before? Did you get a little nervous? Wonder how you should act?

I remember when I was about thirteen years old, I was riding in the car with my dad and we saw Terry Cummings drive by us. At the time he was a Milwaukee Buck (NBA basketball player for you who are uninformed), and I was a huge NBA fan. I shouted, "Dad! It's Terry Cummings! Catch up to him!"

Terry Cummings flew by in his Mercedes Benz. My dad drove ninety miles an hour so that I could wave to Terry Cummings.

When we see famous people, royals, we get all goofy.

The same kind of behavior pops up throughout history when it comes to God or the gods. We humans often approach gods, or God, like we are ants fearful of being squashed.

In the Old Testament era the god of a people called the Philistines was Dagon. People who worshiped Dagon lived in fear. At the drop of a hat, a priest of Dagon could say, "I'm disappointed in that guy. Let's burn him over a fire and slowly rotate him so his pain is greater."

No wonder people approached the gods with fear.

The god of the Babylonians, Marduk, demanded that all parents sacrifice their firstborn son. The priest would heat up this huge idol that had a gaping mouth with a huge tongue. They put the baby on the tongue and slid it into the fire. The death of the baby was supposed to appease the god so that he would allow the rest of the people to live.

The god Molok, like Marduk, was angry and vicious. To appease him people would sacrifice their firstborn babies. The idols of Molok were made of brass and heated up from the bottom and their hands were outstretched. That's where the babies were sacrificed as drums played really loudly so the parents wouldn't be too disturbed at the screaming of their children.

Asherah was a goddess of fertility. If you wanted fruitfulness of any kind—fruitfulness in your family, your business, or your land—you had to appease this god. To do this you had to spend outrageous amounts of money on temple prostitutes. It was common for a father concerned about his family to spend a week or two sleeping with a temple prostitute. Spending half of the family's savings to appease the god, coming home with all kinds of diseases. Bringing it to the family because they were scared the god was going to get 'em.

Humans had to know their place when it came to the gods. They thought they deserved to live in fear, to cower before the gods, to have their children taken away, because they were just humans.

Today, the world says you need to know your place in the presence of royalty.

And in the presence of the gods, you better tremble.

The good news is, there's a new sheriff in town. We celebrate his birth each year. This thing called Christmas—it's about the birth of a new King, a new line of royalty, a new kind of god, a different kind of god, who says to his people: "You are a chosen people, a royal priesthood. You don't need to sip and set it down in front of me; you don't need to stand in front of me with your hands clasped. You yourself are royalty."

Amazing.

And the birth of this baby says there is a new day dawning, a new way to be in the presence of the King of kings, in the presence of royalty.

Jesus, when he walked the face of the earth, said, "I no longer call you servants...[i]nstead, I have called you friends, for everything that I learned from my Father I have made known to you" (John 15:15).

The original hearers would have been flabbergasted to hear the words of 1 Peter 2:9: "[Y]ou are a chosen people, a royal priesthood" or of John 15:15: "I no longer call you servants...I have called you friends." Because they would have in mind all the gods that I just described. It was unheard of for a god to say to a person, "You're my friend."

In fact, if we could travel back in time five thousand years and tell people back then about Christmas, when we celebrate a baby who was born so that we might become royalty and friends with God, they would laugh at us. And then they'd probably throw rocks at us.

Unheard of. That God himself would say, "You are a chosen person, royal. You are a friend of God."

Shocking.

Unimaginable.

The author of Hebrews, in chapter 4, verse 16, says, because Jesus has made his followers a royal priesthood, "Let us then approach God's throne of grace with confidence."

There's the contrast I mentioned at the beginning of this chapter.

Because we are friends with Jesus, instead of approaching God in fear and trembling and with horrible sacrifices, we can stand before the throne of God with confidence.

When held next to the pagan gods of old this beautiful reality stands out like a breath of fresh air.

Notice that there's a throne involved. So we're sure we're dealing with royalty here. And we are not dealing with royalty like a queen who wears cute little hats.

We're dealing with the King of kings, the Lord of lords, the creator of the universe. The one that the Bible says spoke the world into existence and whose very breath gives us life. If he didn't keep breathing his spirit into us, we would cease to exist.

The Bible says that at the name of Jesus every knee will bow in heaven and on earth and under the earth; every knee will bow and every tongue will confess that Jesus is Lord. So we're not talking about some second rate, namby-pamby kind of god, we're talking about THE God. The throne is a real throne.

Also notice that this God isn't a fickle god whose throne you must approach with a baby to sacrifice. It isn't a scary throne, where you need to walk on eggshells wondering if you are going to be skewered and turned on a spit over fire. What kind of throne is it? The text says God's throne is a "throne of grace."

It's not a throne of fear.

It's a throne of grace.

Webster's Dictionary defines grace as benevolence, kindness, mercy, charity. These are words that many people just didn't attach to God in the Old Testament and New Testament eras. Even in our era we often think that God is angry, vengeful, and a killjoy. But God's throne is a throne of benevolence and kindness.

Get this. I looked up the Greek word for "grace" in my Greek dictionary. It says that grace is that which brings joy and pleasure to people.

This throne we are talking about is one that brings joy and pleasure to you!

In my Greek dictionary it says this grace creates delight in the recipient.

Grace brings delight to its recipients. Those of us who have received God's grace ought to be happy people at least some of the time. Receivers of grace ought to have some bounce in their step from time to time because the King of kings has said, "Grace unto you, and delight is yours."

Everyone has issues. If you have a pulse, you have issues. But you also have a King who is bigger than your issues. And if you are no longer a rascal, you are no longer stuck in your issues.

There is no need for us to walk in defeat. With help, maybe counseling, maybe a little anti-depressant, maybe some good friends, and the Holy Spirit, we can stand tall, walking in the delight that grace brings. And in the presence of this throne of grace we can stand with confidence!

Boldness.

Surety.

Certainty.

Assurance.

Freely speaking.

Liberty.

You can approach the throne of grace with confidence.

Think about that for a minute—approaching God's throne with confidence. Have you ever been in a situation where you had no confidence?

Can you keep a secret? When I pick up my kids from school, I feel like a fish out of water. I mean you've got five hundred moms mingling and talking, and about six dads, me being one of them. Plus I'm eight feet taller than everybody so I feel like a giant. I have no idea what to do with myself. I don't know how to go up to a woman. I don't know if it's okay to say, "Hi! How are things?" I'm afraid they will be scared of me or think I'm hitting on them.

I get overwhelmed. I can't even look at one person. I get lost in a sea of estrogen and I don't know what to do.

Quite frankly, I don't like it one bit.

If I can avoid it I will. I'll sit in the car and when my kids come, I'll hop out and hug them, wrestle with them, whatever. I just want to stay in my car and have my kids come to me.

There isn't one lick of confidence in me in that situation. Yuck.

Now by way of contrast, there's another place where I am incredibly confident. And that is anywhere around a basketball and a basketball court. I have been playing basketball basically my whole life. When I step on the basketball court and pick up a basketball, I feel like I'm home. I feel like I rule this land; this is my place.

When I'm coaching, I know how to tell kids what to do. I know how to get them to play as a team. I know how to improve their performance, how to encourage them. When I'm playing I know how to shoot, how to dribble, how to pass. I know how to make my teammates better. I know how to post up. I am comfortable and confident.

When I play with the fellas on Friday I am free and relaxed because this is my land. You pick up the kids and I will play with them on the basketball court. That is my place.

There is something freeing about being confident. There is something releasing about being confident. There is something that unleashes the real us when we can stand tall, confident in who we are in the setting we happen to be in.

This is what the author of Hebrews means when he says to approach the throne of grace with confidence. In the presence of the throne of grace, in the very presence of God, is where you belong.

It's your place.

Your land.

Your environment.

You belong in the presence of God, so stand confidently, assuredly, with certainty that you belong there.

Now that's good news.

Really good news.

The scriptures say, "Let us then approach God's throne of grace with confidence."

So far what we've been talking about doesn't involve any action. Just information. "Throne" is a noun; a throne is a thing. "Grace" describes the throne. "With confidence" describes how we can be when we are there. But we're lacking a verb, an action word.

Verbs are words that describe things you do. Things you become. Jesus, the Holy Spirit, and God the Father are all about verbs. God doesn't want us to be stagnant. God wants us to become what he has created us to be.

The life of following Christ is a verb kind of life, a movement kind of life, a becoming, transforming kind of life. So we need a verb to finish this lesson. "Let us then *approach* God's throne of grace with confidence."

Approach.

To move toward.

To come near.

To come closer.

To move toward something.

We are to approach the throne of grace with confidence.

Don't stand at a distance and look at it and say, "Wow, that's cool. Look at that throne. It's a throne with a king. Look at that. Grace. It's mercy and confidence. Wow, confidence is nice."

Don't just look at it. Move toward it!

The scripture doesn't say to just look at the throne. It doesn't say to admire it from a distance. It says to approach it.

Move toward it.

Touch it.

Feel it.

Embrace it.

Come near.

Approach it.

Jesus' half brother, James, says in James, chapter 4, "Come near to God and he will come near to you."

It's all about the verb.

My friends, this is really your work now. I have given you the verb and you've gotta do something with it. Approach that throne, move toward it, run to it, come near. Approach God's throne of grace with confidence.

I heard about a woman who had been trying to get pregnant for five years. After two miscarriages, she felt hopeless. But this woman knew a rascal who was now royalty who decided to approach the throne of grace with confidence. He prayed over her, "Lord, bless this family with a child." At age forty, this woman who had been unable to conceive carried a child to full term and had a baby.

"Let us then approach God's throne of grace with confidence."

My friend Rod said I could share a story about his dad. He told me that when he was a little kid his dad was diagnosed with hepatitis C. At that time the disease was believed to be incurable; it eventually kills you by destroying your liver. But Rod's family knew the King of Rascals, the one who said to the rascals, "You are a chosen people, a royal priesthood; I call you my friends."

So Rod's parents called the elders of the church. They anointed Rod's dad with oil, and prayed over him.

He doesn't have hepatitis anymore.

That incurable disease is gone because God's people approached God's throne of grace with confidence.

An elder, a spiritual leader of our church, was in a local supermarket talking to the cashier. He asked, "How are you doing?" "Well," she said, "my neck hurts." He asked if it was okay if he prayed for her. They approached the throne of grace with confidence right there in the supermarket! Who knew you could do such things? They prayed, and she exclaimed, "My goodness, my neck is healed! It doesn't hurt anymore."

A woman who attends The River had a friend who needed surgery for her shoulder. They said, "Let's approach the throne of grace with confidence." The woman prayed for her friend. She had the sense that a boring, drilling heat went right through the woman's shoulder. The friend went to the doctor, and the doctor said, "You don't need surgery. Your shoulder is healthy."

"Let us then approach God's throne of grace with confidence."

One day some people from The River asked the Lord, "Show us who you want us to pray for in the park." So they went to the park near the church and the Lord led them to a mother and her child. The child had a cracked skull and some other major issue. The people from The River prayed for the kid and left.

Now a person from The River happens to be friends with somebody who lives right by the kid the River folks prayed for. A few days after they had prayed for him they learned from this other person that the kid's doctors were shocked. Guess who no longer had a cracked skull?

Let us approach the throne of grace with confidence.

With boldness.

You are no longer a rascal, you are royalty. And a perk of being royalty is that you can stand in the presence of the almighty King with your back straight, chin up, and ask for what you need.

The Bible says you lack what you need because God is grumpy with you, right? No, it says you don't have what you need because you haven't asked God for it. You can't ask big enough to shock the Lord. So ask bigger!

Here is what I know about you. You are royalty, but because we live in the time between the Garden of Eden (where humans walked with God) and heaven (where we'll live with God forever), we live in a kingdom in conflict. Sometimes we walk in our royal-ness and other times we walk in our rascal-ness.

Some people have issues, others have marriages that stink. There are people whose finances are non-existent. Jobless people. So many people with so many needs. I say to you, approach the throne of grace with confidence.

If your issues are haunting you, ask the Lord to give you what you need. Approach the throne of grace with confidence.

Chapter 4

Be That Priest

I began serving as a pastor at The River in 2004. Before coming to The River I had graduated from the fine institution of Ferris State University, gone to Western Theological Seminary in Holland, Michigan, and worked as a youth pastor at Community Reformed Church in the small town of Zeeland, Michigan. So I've been serving in a pastoral role since 1993.

And still to this day, when someone calls me Pastor Rob, I cringe.

I don't like it.

Maybe it's because the word "pastor" makes me think of my grandmother's pastor, Pastor Bill. Good man, taught the Word, is with the Lord now. But I remember him talking about how frustrated he was with the deacons of his church. One time he talked about how a light bulb in the kitchen ceiling needed to be replaced, he had called the deacons on Tuesday to come and change it, and they hadn't come until Wednesday morning. I remember thinking, "Dude, change it yourself." Pastor Bill wasn't about manual labor.

Or I think of other pastors I experienced while growing up. They were always different from everyone in the congregation.

Always had ties on, for one thing.

I know of one pastor who worked in the garden with a tie on.

They felt called to be different, and part of being different meant they always had to look their best, even while working in the garden.

I want you to experience what happens when people learn you're a pastor. So I'm giving you permission this week, when you introduce yourself to someone new, to tell them you're a pastor. Just watch their reaction.

I was at the Y, meeting some guys I had never met before. The conversation was flowing, I was making new friends. They were swearing a lot. I guess people at the Y swear a lot. Then someone popped the question: "So, what do you do?"

"Well, I'm a pastor at a church downtown."

"Oh. Sorry about my language. Gotta go."

End of relationship. Over. Done.

Telling people you're a pastor is a buzz kill. It just kills future relationships.

Pastor. The word freaks *me* out.

I wanted to encourage myself a little bit 'cuz I am a pastor, been one for a long time, and I am still not comfortable with it. I decided to look into the origins of the word "pastor."

I rediscovered that the root of our modern day word "pastor" goes back thousands of years. Just after the Israelites entered the promised land, God set up a system where certain men (in Old Testament times all the leaders were men) would lead the people to be close with God. Back then they were called priests. Today we're called pastors.

Leading people closer to God—that's a good role. It's a good responsibility to have. So I was a little encouraged.

Then I got discouraged again when I read Leviticus, chapter 10, where it tells about two dudes who were in the priestly role and got ahead of themselves and the Lord struck them down with fire from heaven. I was a little un-encouraged.

As I explored the role of priests in the Old Testament, I discovered that there are hundreds of verses related to priests.

At about ten words to a verse, we're looking at about ten thousand words on training, equipping, and laying out responsibilities for a priest/pastor. Wow. Unfortunately, it's basically the most boring part in your Old Testament. That part where you're like, "I don't *care* how you offer a grain sacrifice. I *don't care* how you offer a burnt offering. *I don't care* how you are supposed to slaughter the bull. *I don't care that you're supposed to put half over here and half over there."* (Which are all part of the instructions given to priests to help people draw closer to God.)

There are all kinds of instructions for priests in the Old Testament. Instructions like, "Take the blood of the bull and put it on the ear lobes and big toes of the priest."

What?

In addition, these verses include description upon description of how the priest should dress. Because their role is separate and specific, they had to have certain tassels on the bottom of their clothes. They even, I am not kidding you, had to wear certain types of underwear.

The priests were given different roles. There was a priest who made the sacrifice, and a priest who cleaned up the mess afterward. (That's a crappy job right there.)

Another priest was the gatekeeper, the one who acted as a guard for the temple.

There were also the tabernacle setter-uppers. (That's my language, not the Bible's.) For a long time the tabernacle, the Israelites' house of worship, was mobile. God gave instructions for the guys who had to build it and put it up so that it would be done the right way.

Some priests kept the treasury.

Others—this was an exciting job—kept the lamps in the temple filled with oil. Yeah! I can't wait for the next time someone at the Y asks what I do. Maybe I'll tell them, "I keep the lamps filled at the temple!" Yet another way to kill the discussion right there.

Thousands and thousands of words in the Old Testament describe the responsibilities of the priests.

These verses also make it clear that not just anyone could be a priest. You had to be of the line of Levi, descended from the first priest, Aaron. You couldn't wake up one day and say, "Hey, I feel called to be a priest." If you weren't of a certain family lineage, you could never be a priest.

And a priest could not have any bodily blemish. You could be a priest to an old age, but the moment you showed a stoop, you had to retire, because to be a priest was very special.

In fact, modern day Jews today still cling to this. They want to make sure their priests, their rabbis, come from the Levitical line, the line of Levi. They actually do blood tests today to authenticate the lineage.

I've given you a lot of stuff on priests, and that was just the Cliff Notes version. Could you imagine reading all ten thousand words at once? Egad.

Let's pick up our topic of rascals to royalty in Leviticus, chapter 9.

What we have in Leviticus 9 is actually verse 773 of instructions for priests. The former 772 verses laid out all of the priests' great responsibilities, all of these things they have to do, all of the worship services, all the songs to sing, all the different sacrifices to make, how to dress, who could be a priest, etc. When we get to Leviticus 9, we finally see the very first action that the Old Testament priests ever took.

Up to this point the verses on the priesthood simply told them what they were to do in the future. In verse 773 on priesthood we see the first action the priest ever did. There would never be another moment like it. It was the first time the priests acted in their role as priests, and we get to see the first thing they ever did. It is an exciting moment. All this talk about blood and underwear and finally we get to some action.

So what do you think they did? They've got blood on their ear lobes and big toes and their underwear in place. They are ready to go.

You might think their first act would be to worship and celebrate, strike up the band and sing, right? "God is good, praise the Lord," right?

Nope.

Here's the first act these priests performed in Leviticus 9:1:

> On the eighth day Moses summoned Aaron and his sons and the elders of Israel. He said to Aaron, "Take a bull calf for your sin offering and a ram for your burnt offering."

That's it.

No worship.

No haste to praise God. Rather, kill a bull for your sin offering.

Do you see the power and profundity of this first act of the first priest ever?

Do you?

No.

I didn't either at first. Made no sense to me. I would expect anything other than killing a bull.

What if I put it this way: The very first act that the very first priest ever did was to confess his own sin before the Lord and do what was necessary to make himself right before the King of kings.

Ohhhh. Now I see.

This actually is profound. The first thing that the first priests ever did was get right before God. It was because they knew that even though there were 772 verses telling them how to go about being a priest, the priestly role was about a lot more than simply doing external things. In fact, it was mostly about internal things. For priests to do their job well, they had to be right with the King of kings.

A priest who is not right with the King of kings is a worthless priest.

So the priests' first act was to make a sacrifice for their own sins because blood had to be spilled for their sinfulness. If they weren't right before God, they'd be useless to the people.

This is a scary role that these priests had. If they were a little off, if they were a little selfish, if they were a little lust-filled, if they were a little greedy, just a bit me-centered, if they let their sin get in the way, the Lord would say no to whatever they were asking God for on behalf of the people.

In this first act God was saying, "The priestly role is too important for you to not be right with me."

A priest's calling was a call to live a holy life—not a perfect life, but a life wholly given to serving God and obeying what God told them to do.

You may have heard that the head priest, who was called the high priest, went once a year on the Day of Atonement into the Holy of Holies, the most inner room of the Jewish tabernacle. Before he did this, he would tie a rope around his ankle and leave the end of it trailing outside the Holy of Holies. He did this because if he had not made himself right before the Lord before going in, God would strike him dead, and the other priests would have to pull his dead body out by the rope. God did not take the sins of his priests lightly. God does not take the sins of today's pastors lightly either.

Now you know the first act of the priests. Very cheery act, isn't it?

Their second act, after confessing their sins and getting right before the Lord, was to say to the people of Israel, "You need to get right before the King of kings." Still no worship, no clapping, no dancing in praise. Their second act was to look at the people and say, "You are in need of making an offering for your sin."

The priest knew that the sin of the people stunk before the Lord and that the Lord had given them a way to get right before him. Moses tells the priests:

> Then say to the Israelites: "Take a male goat for your sin offering."

This is followed by several verses of careful instruction on how the people were to go about preparing themselves to confess their sin to the Lord.

The priests' role was to challenge people about their sins and then carefully instruct them on what they needed to do to get right before the Lord.

The instructions on how to prepare those offerings were incredibly detailed. This was so that they could offer it rightly before the Lord so that the people themselves would be right before God. The priests took great care and paid attention to every detail so that the people could be right before the Lord.

Leviticus 9:22 tells us the third thing that happened. Aaron, the high priest, lifted his hands toward the people and blessed them.

He blessed them.

The priestly role wasn't a self-serving role, it was all about blessing the people. In the book of Numbers, chapter 6, we can read the blessing the Lord gave to Moses to give to Aaron to bless the people with:

> The Lord bless you and keep you; the Lord make his face shine on you and be gracious to you; the Lord turn his face toward you and give you peace.

This is a good blessing.

Let's recap the three things priests did: they confessed their sins, they led the people to confess their sins, and they blessed the people. And then what happened? Check this out. Verse 24 says that after the priests confessed their own sins, led the people to confess their sins, and blessed the people:

> Fire came out from the presence of the Lord and consumed the burnt offering and the fat portions on the altar. And when all the people saw it, they shouted for joy and fell facedown.

When the priests functioned as they were called to function, the glory of the Lord came down and shone all around and the Lord's people experienced joy.

That's kinda cool.

The priests didn't stay front and center and say, "Look at me." They did their thing and got out of the way. When they got out of the way the Lord's glory came down and the people's joy rose up.

That's pretty cool.

It's what happens when the priests do their work and then get out of the way. (The text actually says that Aaron "stepped down.")

In this section we have been looking at 1 Peter, chapter 9.

First we looked at the fact that you are a chosen people, a royal priesthood. You are chosen, God loves you, and you are no longer a rascal. He's lifted you up and calls you royal.

Then we looked at a couple of perks that have come with that royalty. We looked at the fact that we can live victoriously. The things that used to defeat us don't have to defeat us anymore. That's a great perk.

We looked at standing before the throne of grace with confidence and boldness. No need for us to approach God timidly with fear. Boldness is the word for us!

There's one more thing I want to say to you before we land this plane.

You are priests!

Royal priests.

"You are a chosen people, a royal *priesthood*."

You are a priest.

If you are a follower of Christ I am talking to you. I'm talking to those of you who love Jesus and know Jesus.

Hear this: the responsibilities of the priests in the Old Testament have transferred over to people like you and me.

My role as a pastor is simply to tell you who you are and what you are called to do.

Our verse from First Peter is not a verse for paid pastors. No, it is a verse for Christ followers.

You are the ones who advance God's kingdom.

You are the ones who have a priestly responsibility.

Here's the deal: the kingdom of God will not advance until God's people—that's you and me—get busy and do the work of the kingdom.

We live in the Age of Churchianity. The Age of the Pew Potatoes. This has got to change.

Some of us are busy carrying out our priestly duties, but many of us are just plain lazy.

Because of my own tendency to fall into spiritual laziness, I know it's true for many of you too. To all of you priests, I am telling you right now, you have a responsibility.

"You are a royal priesthood."

I am going to lay it out for you, plain as day.

Your first responsibility as a priest is to confess your sins before the Lord and to get right before the King of kings.

I want you to hear this from the book of Proverbs, chapter 14, verse 9: "Fools mock at making amends for sin."

Fools mock at making amends for sins. We are fools if we don't make our sins right before the Lord.

Here is how we do that: we have to slaughter a bull, put blood on our earlobes and on our toes…

No!

We simply go before Jesus and say, "I am glad you were the last sacrifice. I need your blood to forgive me. Thank you for your forgiveness. Here is where I have sinned and fallen short. I am in need of your grace."

We don't have to wait for forgiveness; it's already here. God's waiting for our repentance. We need to repent, my friends.

Like the priests of old, the first thing we need to do is get right with the King of kings. We are sinful people.

Praise God our sins are covered by the grace of the King of Rascals.

Secondly, our role as priests is to lead people to confess their sins.

Notice how the priests of the Old Testament carefully followed God's instructions on what to do so people could be right before the Lord.

They took a lot of time to do everything just right and they did it with great care.

Today we need to be just as careful.

Here's an example of not taking care with this responsibility: "You're going to hell without Jesus. You need to know Jesus, loser!"

Of course you would never be that extreme, but my point is this: people are turned off by the church of Jesus, and therefore turned off from Jesus, because of our stupidity and lack of care when it comes to presenting the good news about who Jesus really is and what he wants for his followers.

The priests of old had careful instructions and they went about their business very carefully. We need to follow their example. Being careful means your timing is crucial. When all the guys at the Y are swearing it's not smart for me to walk in and say, "Heyyy, I'm Pastor Rob. Watch your mouth or you'll go to hell."

It's careful for me to just relate with them, laugh with them, befriend them. Then, in the course of time, tell 'em about Jesus and what he has done for me and what he wants to do for them.

Careful. But still there's gotta be instruction. You can't be so careful you don't bring the instruction, right? The priests were careful. Detailed. Yet they didn't get lost in caring for the details and miss the instructing.

That uncle who doesn't know Jesus.

Or that neighbor who is far from the Lord.

Or the lady in the next cubicle.

Or the student in your class.

There are a lot of blessings they are missing because they have not repented and turned to Jesus.

They need you to help them on their journey with God.

You are a chosen people, a royal priesthood, every one of you.

No one who is a Christ follower is excluded.

You all are priests.

Confess your sins.

Lead others to confess their sins.

And…remember the third thing the priests did? They blessed the people.

We live in a world full of people who are just longing for somebody to bless them. We live in such a me-centered world.

The priestly role appears radical in our culture. Our call as priests is to bless people.

Bless them!

That money you've got isn't all for you. Bless people with it.

That time in your Outlook calendar is not all yours; give some of your time.

Give your smile, your handshake, your eye contact, your acknowledgement that someone is a human being.

Bless someone, somehow.

Bless them.

Bake them cookies. (Unless you are a bad baker; then don't make them cookies.)

Cut their grass.

Have them over for dinner.

Make it your work to figure out how you can bless the people in your world.

Bless them.

Bless them and then get outta the way. Don't bless them and say, "Look how much I blessed you."

Bless them and then get outta the way.

When we bless people in our culture, even if we don't say a word, when we bless them with love, with time, with our gifts, they will hear, "The Lord bless you and keep you; the Lord make his face shine on you and be gracious to you; the Lord turn his face toward you and give you peace."

Bless them.

Priests in the Old Testament did their work—they confessed, they led the people to confess, they blessed the people—and then what?

The glory of the Lord fell.

Your city will be a different place when you do your priestly work, because the glory of the Lord will fall and the joy of the people will rise!

If you do your work, the Lord will come and do his work, and the joy of the people will rise.

When the glory of God comes, joy goes through the roof.

Joy increases when people encounter the Lord, and people encounter the Lord when the priests are doing their work.

So, priests, get busy and do your work.

You are no longer a rascal.

God has chosen you to be a royal priest.

Be that priest.

That royal priest.